# TIM'S

## A TALE OF RUST AND CORRUPTION

MIKE TURVIL

## Copyright Notice


ISBN-13:979-8-63-866993-5
ISBN-10:8-63-866993-3

To Barry
Best Wishes

DEDICATED TO CLASSIC CAR ENTHUSIASTS EVERYWHERE

## CONTENTS


| | | |
|---|---|---|
| CHAPTER 1 | GENESIS OF A DREAM | 1 |
| CHAPTER 2 | THE RIDE OF A LIFETIME | 9 |
| CHAPTER 3 | THE ARCH VILLIAN | 17 |
| CHAPTER 4 | THE MYSTERIOUS BUS STOP | 25 |
| CHAPTER 5 | AN AMAZING DISCOVERY | 33 |
| CHAPTER 6 | HOW MUCH? | 41 |
| CHAPTER 7 | A DREAM COME TRUE | 49 |
| CHAPTER 8 | THE LABOURS OF HERCULES | 57 |
| CHAPTER 9 | THE WAITING GAME | 65 |
| CHAPTER 10 | LIVING THE DREAM | 75 |
| CHAPTER 11 | GOING ON HOLIDAY | 83 |
| CHAPTER 12 | CATASTROPHE IN PAIGNTON | 91 |
| CHAPTER 13 | THE JOURNEY HOME | 99 |
| CHAPTER 14 | THE DRIVING LESSON | 107 |
| CHAPTER 15 | A LITTLE DRIVE IN THE CAR | 115 |
| CHAPTER 16 | AN END TO THE DREAM | 125 |
| CHAPTER 17 | A CHANGE OF OWNERSHIP | 135 |
| CHAPTER 18 | THE END OF THE ROAD | 143 |
| CHAPTER 19 | THE PRESENT DAY | 151 |
| | APPENDIX | 161 |
| | ABOUT THE AUTHOR | 167 |

1

# GENESIS OF A DREAM

When Bill purchased his brand new Ford Anglia Super in August 1964, it immediately became the most important thing in his life. He would always remember that Saturday morning when he had first caught sight of the car that was going to be his.

He had driven his wife and kids to Salisbury to go shopping and was gradually getting more cheesed off by the minute. His wife Deidre seemed to be intent on dragging him into every single shop on the High Street and their two boys, Colin and Christopher, were being fractious and playing up even more than usual. At eight and seven years old respectively, they were too young to be left at home on their own, so Bill had no choice but to bring them along, not that he had wanted to come shopping either.

This was before the days of the big out of town supermarkets and Deidre would normally buy food and essentials for the family on a daily basis, just as her mother did before her. They lived in the village of Durrington, which is about ten miles north of Salisbury, and the local shops there could provide more or less everything the family needed. A trip to Salisbury, with its wide selection of all kinds of different shops, was something of a treat for her and she had every intention of making the most of it. Bill would have been quite happy to let her go on her own, but Deidre couldn't drive and refused to come in by bus, because of the difficulties involved in struggling with heavy shopping bags.

The family's current means of transport was a 1954 Standard Eight. It had served them well but wasn't new when Bill bought it and now had a tendency to break down far too often. Like most men of his generation, he was reasonably handy with a tool kit and could generally repair most of the things that went wrong, but it had become necessary to buy several replacement parts recently and having to fork out money on new bits for an old car that was past its best didn't seem to make a lot of sense. What he really wanted was a new car, one that he could just jump in and drive, confident in the knowledge that it would get him to wherever he was going without breaking down. But new cars weren't cheap and with Bill being the only breadwinner in the family and two growing boys to feed and clothe, there wasn't all that much money to go around, certainly not enough to spend on luxuries like a new car. So Bill dreamed on, hoping that Lady Luck might smile on him one day and that something would happen that could turn his dream into a reality.

Colin had just grabbed hold of Christopher's teddy bear and was in the middle of trying to tear its ears off when Bill came out of his daydream and saw what the little brat was doing.

'Stop that!' he shouted, 'and give him back his teddy. You wouldn't like it if I did that to your Lenny the Lion puppet.'

Colin chose to ignore his father, even though he knew he would probably get a clip round the ear for doing so.

He threw the teddy down on the pavement and then stamped on it with his foot. Colin didn't need to be told what it meant when Bill began to raise his hand and he closed his eyes, fully expecting to get hit and knowing that it was going to hurt. When nothing happened, he cautiously opened them again to find out why.

Bill was standing there with one arm raised as if he had been frozen in time. There was a strange look on his face. A beam of sunlight had just broken through the clouds and after reflecting off the enormous glass window fronting a car showroom on the other side of the road, it had hit him in the eyes and was now lighting up his face. Momentarily dazzled, he had paused in mid swing, which is why Colin had been reprieved.

'Why are you just standing there like that?' Deidre asked. 'Clout the lad. You know he deserves it.'

Bill slowly lowered his arm and turned to face his wife. 'I think I've just had an epiphany!' he told her. 'I must go across the road to see what's behind that glass window.'

Deidre started to get annoyed and Colin couldn't believe his luck, although this was short lived. Deidre whirled round to face him and smacked him hard. He immediately burst into tears. Christopher laughed when this happened but her dander was well and truly up by now and she clouted him as well for good measure. Now both boys were crying and passersby were beginning to stare. She turned back to shout at Bill but he had walked off. He was now half way across the road, seemingly oblivious to the traffic, and was heading for the car dealership on the other side. She grabbed both boys by the hand and stormed across the road in pursuit of her husband.

By now Bill had somehow managed to cross the road safely and was standing with his face pressed against the dealer's window. The glare from the glass made it hard for him to see through it, but he knew there was something there he needed to see. It was as if he could hear a voice in his head and that voice was calling to him, 'You must come and look at me!' He walked over to the open door and entered the showroom.

There were various cars displayed inside but Bill knew exactly which one had called to him. It was a light blue Ford Anglia Super, with a white roof and chrome trimmed white stripes along both sides. It was gleaming under the fluorescent lights strategically placed across the ceiling and all its shiny chrome trim sparkled, as if with a life of its own. The hooded headlights and the backward sloping rear window gave the car a futuristic look and the full width front grille fitted in with this as well. It even had raised rear fins, just like the American cars of that time, with chromed light clusters at the ends. Bill was smitten. It was love at first sight and he knew this was the car of his dreams. He walked around it slowly, taking in every detail of its appearance. This quickly attracted the attention of a dangerous predator, the man whose job it was to try to sell the cars in that showroom.

'She's a beauty, isn't she?' the salesman said, after carefully positioning himself between Bill and the showroom's open door. Car sales had been a bit slow recently and he didn't want to see this potential customer escape.

'Absolutely fantastic,' Bill replied. 'How much is it?'

'Let me show you the inside and explain some of the Anglia Super's features,' the salesman said, skilfully avoiding having to answer Bill's question at such an early point in the negotiations.

A disturbance near the door caused him to pause momentarily and he turned in that direction. A woman had just entered the showroom and was dragging two screaming brats in with her as well. They didn't look like potential customers to Charlie and he would have ignored them, but for the noise the two boys were making. It was the last thing he needed when he was just about to launch into his carefully prepared sales pitch and he knew that he would have to do something about them. Opening the driver's door, he suggested that Bill sit inside to experience the comfortable driving position. This invitation was immediately accepted and with Bill now engrossed with the wonders of the Anglia's interior, he could safely leave him for the moment and go and deal with that woman and her kids. He stopped off on his way over to them to pick up a couple of fruit lollypops from the jar on his desk. Long experience had taught him that the best way to shut kids up was to give them something to keep them occupied like a gob stopper. The lollypops were just the thing.

'Good morning, Madame,' he said. 'I am currently dealing with a customer, but if you and your children would like to take a seat for a moment, then I will get back to you as soon as possible.' He held up the two lollypops for the boys to see and having gained their attention, walked across the showroom to a seating area on the far side. Colin and Christopher trailed behind him, each with an outstretched hand. Deidre understood why he was doing this but then just shrugged and joined them. She wasn't about to let this salesman start putting ideas in her husband's head, but at least he had got the boys to stop crying. She would allow Bill a few minutes to drool over that car he seemed so interested in, but then she would step in and put a stop to all this tomfoolery.

'It has wind up windows,' Bill remarked, when the salesman returned to him. 'My old car has only got the ones that slide backwards and forwards.'

'Yes it has,' Charlie responded, 'and the gearbox has synchromesh on all four forward gears. It has a heater that comes as standard and electric windscreen wipers, not like the vacuum ones that they fitted to the Anglia 100E. They used to slow down whenever the car sped up, if you remember. Windscreen washers and a cigar lighter are also standard fittings on this model and you can even open the bonnet from inside the car.'

'Wow! They seem to have thought of everything.'

'Well, this is the Super you are looking at and it has refinements you just wouldn't get on the Deluxe model and many more features that aren't on the basic model. The Super also has the benefit of an 1198 cc engine, so it has more power than any of the previous versions.'

'Does it come with a starting handle?' Bill asked. 'I often have to use one to get my old car going when it won't start in the mornings.'

'You will never need a starting handle with this car, sir. It is so beautifully engineered that it will start every time on the turn of a key. You will have no worries on that score because it was designed to be a hundred percent reliable.'

'So it doesn't have a starting handle?'

'There isn't even a hole where you could put a starting handle, sir. Ford are so confident that one will never be needed.'

‘So why does the back window slope inwards? I’ve never seen one like that on a car before.’

‘That is another piece of clever engineering, sir. It will stop rain collecting on the rear window and you will always be able to see clearly out the back.’

‘So how much does this shining monstrosity cost?’ a female voice enquired. Deidre had decided that she’d left Bill with the salesman for long enough and come to join them.

‘That’s the wife,’ Bill said, as if that was all that needed to be said.

‘I’m sorry, Madame,’ Charlie said, now on the back foot. ‘I didn’t realise that you were with this gentleman. So those fine young lads over there are yours are they, sir?’

Bill gave a grunt to signify his acceptance of that fact.

‘Well the Ford Anglia Super is just the thing for a family of four, with loads of room in the back for when your boys start getting bigger.’

‘You still haven’t said how much it costs,’ Deidre was not going to be put off.

Salesmen recognise when they are batting on a losing wicket and Charlie knew he would have to reveal the price, even though he didn’t want to do so just yet. ‘This Anglia Super could be yours for the bargain price of £575 10s 5d, including purchase tax,’ he told them. If you don’t want to pay the full amount immediately, we could even arrange easy terms for you.’

Bill was visibly startled to hear the price of the car, as it was almost half of what hc earned in a year. Deidre’s reaction was even more spectacular. Her mouth dropped open and she was totally dumfounded for the moment. Then, in a voice filled with incredulous disbelief, she said, 'How much? You've got to be joking!'

## 2

## THE RIDE OF A LIFETIME

Three minutes later and the entire family were back out on the street. Deidre had just shouted, 'We're leaving!' and the two boys scuttled for the door as if their lives depended on them getting there quickly. She had to virtually drag Bill out of the car, but then propelled him towards the door as well. Charlie had just about enough time to press some Anglia sales literature into Bill's hand before he was out of the showroom. He had felt convinced that there was a good chance of him making a sale before Deidre stuck her oar in, but it seemed she wore the trousers in that family and she was definitely not the sort of woman he wanted to argue with.

From just outside the open doorway, Bill glanced back at the Anglia and a trick of the light made it appear as if the offside headlight switched itself on and off again for a moment. It gave him the distinct impression that the car had winked at him.

There was very little conversation for the rest of their shopping trip and even the two boys seemed to have very little to say. Bill had a faraway look in his eyes and Deidre was still trying to get over the shock of hearing the price of the Anglia. Five hundred and seventy-five pounds was more money than she had ever had in her life and to think that Bill would even consider spending that much on a car was the most ridiculous thing she'd ever heard. She had no doubts in her mind that he was thinking just that, as the expression on his face told her everything she needed to know. He wanted that car, it was as simple as that, and he was busy trying to work out how he could buy it.

The old Standard didn't want to start when they got back to the car park and Bill ended up having to crank it into life with the starting handle. Eventually it fired up and they were able to head for home, but this was the last straw for Bill. He really hated the old banger now and knew that he would never be satisfied until he could take possession of the beautiful Ford Anglia Super that had called out to him from across the other side of the road.

That Saturday evening found Deidre sitting watching 'Dixon of Dock Green' on the television and Bill studying the literature he had been given by the salesman.

'It says here that the Anglia Super has a top speed of eighty-two miles per hour,' he told Deidre. 'I'm lucky if I can get more than fifty-five out of the old Standard.'

'Who on earth would want to go that fast?' she responded. Deidre had decided there was no harm in letting him read the literature and daydream about owning that car, as there was no way they could possibly afford to buy it. He had to know that as well and when he finally accepted the reality of this fact, he would stop going on about his dream car and she would hear no more on the subject. In the meantime, she would just find ways to criticise any plus points he chose to raise.

'It's not so much a question of being able to go fast,' he told her, 'but more one of available power. You know how the Standard struggles to get up hills sometimes, particularly when we're all in it, well that wouldn't happen in the Anglia Super because it has a much more powerful engine.'

'That would mean spending more money on petrol as well,' she threw back, 'and that's five bob a gallon.'

'Not necessarily,' he said. 'Engines have moved on since the Standard was designed and these new more efficient engines are much better on fuel consumption. We could get thirty to the gallon with the Anglia and that would make it cheaper to run than the Standard.'

Deidre realised that her tactic wasn't working, as it looked like he was going to have an answer to her every objection. It was time to deliver the coup de grâce and to pop his balloon once and for all.

'And where are you proposing to find the money to buy this dream machine of yours?'

Her question was met with stunned silence. Bill knew there was no way that he could magic up the required amount and even if they bought it on easy terms; the regular monthly payments would cripple the family's finances, always assuming that they could scrape up the deposit to begin with.

'I guess you're right,' Bill finally said, putting the brochure down next to him on the sofa. Deidre went back to watching her television programme and he didn't say another word about cars for the rest of the evening.

It was inevitable that Bill would dream about the Anglia that night. He was back in the car showroom in Salisbury, but this time he was on his own. Even the salesman didn't seem to be around, so he could stand and admire the car he so much wanted without fear of interruption. He walked towards the Anglia but stopped a short distance away so that he could study the design features that had been built into its front end. It seemed to be wider than he remembered, but the shiny full width chrome trimmed grille, almost as wide as the bumper itself, may just have given that impression. He really liked the hooded headlights and the chrome trim around the front of them reminded him of a pair of eyebrows. It was little wonder that he had thought the car winked at him. The side lights were set into the grille at either side and incorporated blinking indicators, something his Standard didn't have until he put some on to replace the stupid semaphores originally fitted. A badge just forward of the bonnet proudly declared the car to be an Anglia Super and seemed to be a tasteful addition. To Bill's mind, the front of the car oozed style and refinement and there wasn't a thing about it that he would have wished to change.

Suddenly, the Anglia's headlights lit up, although there was no one in the car to turn them on. As such, it took him by surprise, but nothing like as much as when one of the chrome eyebrows began to move. It dropped down slowly to obscure the car's headlight for a moment, before rising back up again to its normal position. There was no doubt about it this time. His dream machine had just winked at him. It was trying to tell him something and he immediately realised what that was, when the driver's side door opened all on its own.

The car was suggesting to him that he should take it out for a drive and as it to reinforce this message; the large glass windows at the front of the showroom began to slide open. Bill walked round to the side of the

Anglia and cautiously climbed in. As he was making himself comfortable in the driver's seat, the car's door closed itself. He looked down at the dashboard and noticed that the light switch was in the 'on' position. Not only that, but that the keys were in the ignition as well. He reached out towards them, but they moved on their own before he could touch them. The engine fired and quickly settled down to a gentle purr. Bill was sitting in a car that had just started itself and the way ahead was now clear for him drive it out of the showroom and onto the road.

He moved his foot towards the clutch pedal, but he needn't have bothered. The pedal moved of its own accord and first gear was selected by an invisible hand. As the clutch pedal came back up, the throttle moved down slightly and the Anglia began to move. Bill didn't know whether to grab the steering wheel or not, but somehow sensed that this wouldn't be necessary. The Anglia Super was taking him for the ride of his life and all he had to do was to sit back and enjoy it.

Cruising through the deserted streets at night in a car that was driving itself was a very strange experience, but Bill decided that the Anglia had to know what it was doing and gradually began to relax. Even the traffic lights seemed to be helping, as they all changed to green as the car approached them. They were soon out on the open road and the Anglia increased speed until they were buzzing along at nearly seventy miles per hour. The absence of any other vehicles on the road was puzzling and Bill thought it strange that there were no other people about. He would have expected to see the odd person here or there, but he and the Anglia seemed to be all alone in an empty world.

The car proved to be every bit as comfortable as he had expected and the ride was smooth and quiet. There was a certain amount of wind noise when they were travelling at speed, but no drafts invaded the cabin. The old Standard Eight let in the wind through the sliding windows and Bill had got used to being buffeted about by a draft whenever he drove the car. The Anglia took the corners as if it was glued to the road and he was given a demonstration of how effectively the brakes worked, when the Anglia suddenly did an emergency stop for no apparent reason. They had been driving along a country road and were just passing a bus stop when the brakes were applied. Bill couldn't understand why the Anglia had chosen to stop in this particular spot, but there had to be a reason. The car's headlights continued to illuminate the road ahead, but all the surrounding area was still in darkness. He glanced across at the bus stop and it began to glow with an eerie light. Bill found that very unsettling and couldn't explain what he was witnessing. After a minute or two, the Anglia continued on its way, leaving him totally confused.

As he wasn't actually driving the car, Bill could afford to take his eyes off the road and examine its interior. The rear bench seat looked comfortable and was padded at both sides. The blue fitted carpeting on all floor areas perfectly complimented the blue vinyl of the seats and the trapezium shaped instrument and switch cluster in front of him added to the vehicle's space age look. He noticed that this shape was repeated on the passenger side of the dashboard, in the form of a lockable glove box. There was even a storage tray beneath the dashboard, which would come in handy for putting any odd items he might want to carry in the car.

Having a fitted heater was a bit of a novelty for Bill, as the Standard Eight didn't have one. He would need to make a point of telling Deidre about it, as she was always going on about being cold in their car during the winter time. He experimented with its controls and was pleasantly surprised when he felt a blast of warm air around his feet. It was only then that he suddenly noticed that he was still wearing his pyjamas and couldn't imagine why he had left the house wearing them. But come to think of it, he didn't remember leaving the house either.

All too soon, he found himself being driven along the High Street again and upon reaching the dealership; the Anglia carefully reversed itself back into the showroom. The engine stopped, the lights turned themselves off and the driver's door opened. Bill's ride of a lifetime was over, but what a fantastic trip it had been. He now wanted this Ford Anglia Super more than anything else in the world and he didn't care what that might take. This car was going to be his, whatever Deidre had to say about it, and there had to be some way around the problem of him not being able to afford it. The Anglia Super had clearly demonstrated that it wanted Bill to be its new owner and he wasn't about to let it down. They were meant to be together and come hell or high water, he had every intention of making that happen.

## 3

## THE ARCH VILLIAN

In July 1957, the then Prime Minister, Harold Macmillan, declared that the people of the United Kingdom had 'never had it so good'. When this was reported in the papers the following day, the leader of a gang of crooks in London didn't quite see it that way. He had masterminded a number of high profile robberies in the past, but the police were now hot on his heels and it could only be a matter of time before they finally nailed him.

It was getting more difficult to plan a successful bank robbery these days, because of all the extra security precautions in place, and the potential haul from holding up Post Offices often didn't justify the risks involved. London was still a hive of criminal activity, but his problem was that he was too well known in the area. He couldn't afford to take too many chances, but unless he masterminded a major crime in the near future he would lose his credibility in the criminal underworld.

He looked up from his newspaper and said out loud, 'It's all very well for Macmillan to say that we've never had it so good, but I can remember when times were a lot easier for me than they are now.'

Mr X was a lifelong criminal and led a gang of robbers who were quite prepared to use guns. Pointing such a weapon at a terrified bank clerk always ensured their compliance, but it was no good grabbing a huge pile of used notes if you then ran into the Sweeney as you left the bank. The Metropolitan Police Flying Squad also carried guns on occasions and to consider having a shootout with them was bordering on the suicidal.

His other big risk was the narks. Villains who were prepared to tip off the police about future robberies being planned. Quite often, they did this to get themselves off the hook for some crime they'd committed, but others just did it for the money. Mr X had enemies in the criminal underworld and he knew it. Many of them were envious of his success and his would be a big scalp for the police, if they were able to arrest him. Such was his fear of informers that he daren't even bring new members into his gang in case one of them turned out to be a nark, but several gang members had been nabbed recently and he was getting a bit short of manpower for a major robbery.

'The problem,' he told himself, 'is that planning a big job in London is getting riskier all the time. The cops are getting far too hot around here and they will probably hear all about it before we can pull it off.'

He didn't want to spend the rest of his life in jail, but he knew that the police wouldn't kill him, which was more than could be said for some of his enemies and possibly even a number of his criminal associates. He would need to do something to show that he was still at the top of his game.

Later that day, Mr X had a meeting with the number two in his gang, Joe MacNally. An Irishman by birth, Joe was a hulking great brute of a man, with a cauliflower ear and a broken nose, souvenirs from his days in the boxing ring. What he didn't get boxing however was the vivid scar that ran from the bottom of his left ear to the corner of his mouth. His face had been slashed open by a razor, but the man who did it ended up in hospital for six months and could now only walk with the aid of a pair of crutches. Joe was not the sort of man to tangle with and he was totally loyal to Mr. X.

'I just wanted to have a word with you about that bank job we did in Clapham six months ago,' Mr X told Joe. 'The police turned up as we were leaving and would have nailed us for sure, if we hadn't been using the Jags as getaway cars.'

'Yeah,' Joe agreed, 'we were lucky that time, but now the coppers are starting to get Jaguars of their own and that's going to make it harder to outrun them in the future.'

'Have you found out who squealed on us yet?'

'No I haven't, but I promise you I will.'

'And what about Charlie Green? Mr X asked.

'That stupid prat used his share of the loot to buy himself a brand new Rover and the law was onto him like a shot. He knows well enough to keep his mouth shut, but he's going to be inside for at least ten years.'

'So what have we learned from all of this?'

Joe scratched his head in thought and then said, 'I'm not really sure, boss. You're the brains of the outfit, so why don't you tell me.'

Mr X began telling Joe the thoughts he'd been having earlier. He explained how it was now harder than ever to pull off a successful job in London, because of the increased risk of someone ratting on them and the fact that the police seemed to be getting more efficient.

'It's not that they're stupid,' he said. 'We've always

known that, but they are really cracking down on major crime these days and we might all end up in jail unless we're a lot more careful than we have been of late.'

'I've been thinking that as well,' Joe commented. 'But what can we do about it?'

'Well, the first thing is to stop planning jobs in London for a while. It's getting far too chancy and the coppers are just waiting for us to make a mistake. Our gang is well known in this area and there are a lot of people out there who would like to see us banged up.'

'So you're thinking of us doing a big job outside of London?'

'Exactly,' Mr X agreed. 'We go to some place where the cops don't know us and commit a robbery there. Afterwards, we can let it be known in London that we did the job, but if I plan it carefully and we all have cast iron alibis established, then the police will never be able to pin it on us, even if they know we did it, and it will drive them crazy!'

'I like it, boss,' Joe said with a chuckle.

'And the other thing we do,' added Mr X, 'is not share out the money right away, as we've done in the past. We don't want to run the risk of someone like Charlie attracting attention by suddenly starting to spend a lot of money. We will bury it somewhere the cops will never think of looking and then share out the spoils a year or so later, after the heat has died down.'

'Have you got anywhere in mind, boss?'

'As a matter of fact, I have. Our next big job is going to be in Salisbury.'

Albert Entwistle was the manager of the Midland Bank in Salisbury High Street. His was the largest bank in Salisbury, if not the county, and as such was used by virtually all of the major businesses in the area. Friday mornings were always Albert's busiest time, as all the local companies would come in to collect large amounts of bank notes in small denominations, to meet the wages they would be paying out that afternoon. This Friday morning, like any other, the table in the storeroom next door to Albert's office was piled high with stacks of tenners, fivers, pounds and ten bob notes, together with bags of coinage, in readiness for the rush.

At ten thirty precisely, a big van pulled up outside. Eight men jumped out of it and then ran into the bank. They were mostly large men and each wore a stocking over his head. Three of them were carrying shotguns and a number of the others had revolvers. There were only a few customers in the bank at the time and the sudden appearance of this group of armed men caused an immediate panic. Albert rushed out of his office when he heard the commotion and found himself facing a giant of a man. His facial features were obscured by a stocking, but Albert could still see the scar running down the left hand side of his face.

'Do as you're told and you won't get hurt,' the man ordered. Albert had never met an armed bank robber before and was absolutely terrified. He collapsed to the ground and just lay there quivering. He obviously wasn't going to cause the gang any problems.

Five of them rushed off into the storeroom, while the others stayed in the main area, waving their shotguns and revolvers around menacingly and generally intimidating the staff and few customers unfortunate enough to have been in the bank at the time.

In less than three minutes, the men in the storeroom re-emerged, now carrying sacks full of bank notes.

They hadn't bothered to take the bags of coins, as their weight would have been an encumbrance. They took these out to the waiting van and after hurling them into the back, climbed in behind them. The remaining robbers then followed them out, after Joe had warned the petrified men and women still in the bank that if anyone tried to follow them they would be shot.

The entire robbery had taken no more than five minutes and hardly a word had needed to be said. It was as neat a bank job as Mr X could have wished for and only went to prove that with proper planning and a thorough knowledge of the target bank's routines, it was possible to pull off the perfect heist. It was now time to follow the rest of his plan through and to make their escape with the loot.

The van drove to a large barn just outside Salisbury and its double doors swung open to admit the robbers as they approached. Once inside the barn, the gang transferred the sacks of money to a smaller van that was already in there, before jumping into a couple of nondescript cars especially chosen for their anonymity. Leaving just Joe and Mr X there, the rest of the gang then drove off to return to London. No one there would have even realised that they had been away from the city, as the alibis Mr X had prepared for all of them had been very elaborately constructed.

'That went well,' Joe said. 'Not even a sniff of the law and those people in the bank were the most obliging bunch I've ever seen. We hardly even had to threaten them and yet they would have done anything we asked of them.'

'Perhaps we should have told them to fill the sacks for us,' Mr X joked, 'to save us all that physical work.'

They then set about dousing the big van and the inside walls of the barn with petrol. The plan was to fire the barn to remove any possible incriminating evidence they may have left, either at the barn or in the van itself. Joe drove the smaller van outside while Mr X lit the fire. As soon as he was sure it was well alight, he joined Joe in the van outside, after closing the barn's double doors behind him. As the van drove off, flames began licking through the walls of the barn and within a few minutes, it was a blazing inferno.

The next part of Mr X's plan was to hide the money but before he and Joe could do that, it would need to be removed from the sacks and the sacks disposed of. A special location had been arranged where they could do this without being seen and, just as importantly, without arousing any suspicion. At this secret place, the money was transferred to three large suitcases. Mr X had estimated the size of their potential haul, but it was a little more than even he had expected. As such, there wasn't quite enough room for all of it in the suitcases and they ended up with a pile of pound notes and ten bob notes that they would need to burn along with the sacks.

'I never thought that I would ever be burning money literally,' Joe remarked, as he watched the small fire he had just lit, 'but I suppose it's for the best though, as it wouldn't do to have any of those suitcases bursting open.'

Two hours later, Mr X took off in a small private plane from an old airfield in the Wiltshire countryside. If the police ever investigated where he was at the time of the robbery, they would discover that he wasn't even in the country. Joe's alibi was that he was visiting his ailing mother in Liverpool and there would be any number of witnesses prepared to come forward and swear under oath that he arrived there three days before the robbery took place and never left his mother's side for a whole week.

At the bank, a now recovered Albert had just finished working out how much money had actually been taken. He estimated the total to be around seventy-eighty thousand pounds (the equivalent of one point six million in today's terms). Mr X had chosen his target well and the gang had pulled off their biggest robbery ever.

In order to avoid detection, Mr X's pilot flew fast and low over the sea on their way to France. When the plane's single engine failed, they were far too low for him to have the time to do anything about it and they plummeted into the sea at one hundred and fifty miles per hour. Both he and Mr X were killed instantly.

Joe returned to London on the Wednesday following the robbery. On the way to his local pub that evening, he was ambushed by three men from a rival gang. They were not prepared to take any chances with a man the size of Joe and all three emptied their guns into him, just to make sure.

Mr X and Joe were the only two members of the gang who knew where the money from the bank robbery was hidden and they took that secret with them to their graves.

# 4

# THE MYSTERIOUS BUS STOP

Seven years later, Deidre was berating Bill at the breakfast table. 'What on earth were you thinking about last night? You were tossing and turning so much that I hardly got a wink of sleep.'

'I had the most wonderful dream,' he told her. 'I went out for a ride in that Ford Anglia Super in Salisbury and we went all round the area with it driving itself.'

'I might have known that car would come into it somewhere. I thought you might have got it out of your system by now, seeing as how we can't possibly afford to buy the thing.'

'I know that,' he said, 'but there's no harm in me dreaming about owning it.' He had no intention of telling her about the promise he had made to himself in his dream. That wonderful car was going to be his one day and he meant it, but he didn't have the vaguest idea how to bring this about.

He had checked his pools coupon the previous evening, in the hope that he might have successfully predicted eight score draws, but he'd only managed to pick one correct result. 'What a waste of a shilling that was,' he told himself, but he knew he would need an awful lot of shillings if he wanted to buy the Ford Anglia Super.

As it was promising to be a nice sunny day, Bill

decided to take the family out for a picnic that afternoon. Sundays were about the only day he could do this and a bit of fresh air wouldn't do the boys any harm at all. Deidre was quite happy to go along with this suggestion and set about planning what things she would need to get ready to take on their picnic.

Colin and Christopher were enthusiastic about the proposed outing and wanted to know if their dad planned on stopping off at the railway station while they were out. Like all young boys their age, they were keen train spotters and the pedestrian bridge across the tracks at Salisbury station was the perfect vantage point to watch the trains pass by underneath them in both directions. Some obviously stopped at the station itself and this provided them with the opportunity to see some huge steam locomotives close up, as they sat by the platform belching out smoke and steam and making the most incredible noises. It would be four years before the last steam trains ran on the country's main lines and the boys were too young to appreciate that what they were seeing was the end of an era.

'Of course we will stop at the station,' he told them. 'Your mother will probably stay in the car and do her knitting, but I'm sure she won't mind if we spend half an hour or so watching the trains from the bridge. You pair had better behave yourselves though, because if I get a repeat of the way you were acting up yesterday, then I'll call the whole thing off and we will never go to the station again.

Deidre smiled when she heard this. That threat was enough to ensure that the boys would be as good as gold all day. She carried on making sandwiches in the kitchen.

Bill wasn't all that fussed about watching trains, but knew how enthusiastic his two young sons were. He had given them a notebook in which to record train numbers and even bought them an ABC Train Spotter's Guide, so that they could tick off any that they saw. It was sometimes difficult to keep them entertained and out from under his feet, so this passing interest of theirs suited him quite well. One thing he also planned to do while they were out was to visit that bus stop. He was intrigued as to why the Anglia had decided to stop there and was hoping to pick up some clue if he had a look at the place in daylight.

He hadn't been paying a lot of attention to the route the car had taken in his dream, but knew that the bus stop was close to the sign for Elm Tree Farm, as he had seen this as they went by. A few minutes searching his Ordinance Survey map was all it took to locate this particular farm and he now knew that it was on the A360, just a few miles north of the city. That would be easy enough to get to, as he would only need to join the A303 just south of Durrington and then head west. A left turn at the crossroads a mile or so beyond Stonehenge would put him on the A360 and he could then drive south towards Salisbury until he reached the farm sign. The bus stop he was looking for was within a hundred yards or so of that signpost, so it shouldn't be all that difficult to find.

A couple of hours later, Bill stopped the car by the sign for Elm Tree Farm and got out. He had either just driven past the bus stop without seeing it, or they hadn't reached it yet. He glanced back in the direction they'd come from and decided that it had to be the other way, probably just a short distance further on. He got back into the car to continue driving along the road.

'Why have we stopped here, Daddy?' Christopher asked. 'Is this where we are going to have our picnic?'

Deidre was also wondering what he was up to and was about to query this when he said, 'I'm just looking for something. It shouldn't take me a minute.'

He proceeded slowly in the car but then came to a halt again, next to a bus shelter on the left hand side of the road. It had just been a single pole with a metal flag at the top in his dream, but this one had a brick shelter around it. It couldn't possibly be the same one.

A woman was walking by with her dog and so he stopped her and asked whether she lived locally. When she confirmed that she did, he went on to ask if there were any other bus stops close by. 'That's the only one for a couple of miles in either direction,' she told him, 'but the bus drivers often stop to pick up or drop off passengers pretty much anywhere along this road.'

'How long has it had a shelter around it?' I seem to remember that it used to be just a bus stop with a pole.'

'The council built that thing five years ago,' she said. 'Waste of good money if you ask me, as no one ever uses it.' Bill thanked the woman for her help and watched as she strolled off, with the dog following on behind.

Deidre had got out of the car by now and walked over to where he was standing. 'So what is this sudden interest you've developed in bus stops? There's an extremely pretty one in our village, if you're starting to get a fetish about bus stops and bus shelters.'

'No,' he said slowly. It's just this particular one that interests me.'

He was understandably confused, but knew there had

to be some sort of explanation. He looked up and down the road in both directions and from what he could see; this definitely appeared to be the right spot. He decided to investigate the bus stop more closely and stepped into the shelter. As he did so, he began to feel a strange sensation. It was as if he was dreaming again and he suddenly realised that two men were standing right there next to him. The shorter of the two was fairly nondescript but the other fellow was a veritable giant of a man, with a long scar down the side of his face. The shelter had somehow disappeared and all that was there now was the bus pole with its flag on the top.

'We will put the ticket in this biscuit box and bury it right here by the bus stop,' the smaller man said. 'It will be quite safe there until we come back to get it after the heat's died down.'

The men seemed totally oblivious to Bill's presence and began digging a hole some short distance away from the bus stop. They dropped the biscuit box the smaller man was carrying into it and then filled in the hole again. After that, they walked back to a small van that was parked by the side of the road and after throwing their spade in the back, drove off.

'Are you alright?' Deidre was shouting into Bill's ear. 'You're standing there like you're in a trance or something. Wake up you stupid idiot!'

Bill shook his head to try and clear it. He felt decidedly whoozy and didn't know what had just happened to him. Deidre was standing beside him and his car with the kids in it was still parked where he'd left it. There was no sign of the two men or their van and the bus stop now had the shelter around it again.

'I just had a funny turn,' he told his wife. 'Give me a

minute or two and I'll be as right as rain again.'

Deidre had a concerned look on her face, but he seemed to be coming out of it now, so she walked over to the car and got back in.

Bill glanced across at the spot where the men had been digging and began to wonder. He knew he didn't have a spade in the car and mentally went through the contents of the toolbox he always carried in the boot of the Standard, trying to remember whether there was anything in it that might serve the same purpose. Nothing immediately came to mind. He knew that the big man had dug quite a deep hole, so it would be no good scrabbling away at the ground with his hands. He would definitely need a spade if he wanted to find out whether something was buried there, so there was nothing he could do at this particular moment. He walked back to the car.

The picnic was great fun and all the family enjoyed sitting there on the car blanket tucking into the food that Deidre had prepared. There were fish paste and cheese and tomato sandwiches, together with ham rolls and slices of pork pie. She had also brought along some apples and a small bunch of bananas. The boys washed down their meals with Tizer and Deidre drank milk. Bill was pleasantly surprised to see that she had thought to put two half pint bottles of light ale in the hamper for him. When everyone had eaten their fill, they put the used dishes and cutlery, together with the empty bags and wrappers back into the hamper, which was then returned to the car.

At Salisbury railway station, Bill bought three one penny platform tickets and led the boys up onto the pedestrian bridge to watch the trains. Deidre stayed in the car, as he had fully expected her to do. He couldn't get the strange vision he'd had out of his mind and was desperately trying to work out what it was supposed to mean. He'd thought it odd when the Anglia had decided come to an abrupt halt by the bus stop in his dream, but what had happened when he actually stood in the same place seemed even weirder. The answer had to have something to do with whatever was buried in that hole, if there was anything buried there at all, but he certainly intended to find out. He would need to go to work tomorrow, but he planned to take a spade with him and nip out during his lunch hour. He was going to go back to that bus stop and do a bit of excavating.

The boys were absolutely thrilled when an enormous steam locomotive stopped in the station and Bill noticed that the carriages were being detached, in readiness for moving them to one of the sidings. This meant that the train was going to be there for a while, so he took Colin and Christopher down to the platform so that they could have a closer look at it. Their joy at being right next to such a massive steam engine turned to elation, when the train driver invited the lads to come up and join him on the footplate. As Bill helped each of them down afterwards, the driver gave him a broad wink. He was probably still a kid at heart. Bill knew that the boys would be talking about this for weeks to come and that all their schoolmates were going to be green with envy.

All in all, the day had turned out very well indeed and everyone slept soundly when they all went to bed that night. It took Bill quite a while to drop off, as he couldn't stop thinking about what might be buried next to that bus stop. He knew he needed to find out, but supposing he did uncover a biscuit tin, what would he find inside it? The man had mentioned a ticket, but what did the ticket relate to? He realised that this event he had somehow managed to witness must have taken place more than five years ago, as the bus shelter wasn't actually built until 1959, according to what the woman with the dog had told him, and it hadn't been there in his vision. It was indeed an intriguing mystery but what puzzled him most, was what on earth did it all have to do with that Ford Anglia Super he had set his heart on?

## 5

## AN AMAZING DISCOVERY

At lunchtime the following day, Bill told his supervisor that there was something he needed to do and that he might be a bit late back from lunch. He had worked for this company for many years and was a well respected employee, so the supervisor didn't have a problem with this.

Back at the bus stop, Bill took his spade from the car and after carefully checking to make sure there was nobody around to see what he was doing, began digging in the same spot that the men in his vision had done. It was a warm day and the work proved to be quite tiring. When he had dug down about two feet, he heard the spade strike something solid and proceeded more carefully after that. A few minutes later and he could see the outline of some sort of box in the hole. He reached down to get hold of it and with a little bit more clearing away with the spade, was finally able to lift out his prize. It was definitely a metal box and the outside of it was very rusty. A quick glance at his watch told him that he was running out of time, so he put the box to one side and quickly filled in the hole again. After smoothing it over to try to disguise the fact that the soil in the area had been disturbed, he returned to the Standard with the tin.

He desperately wanted to examine it straightaway, but

knew that he couldn't spare the time. It was already well past the hour when he should have been back at work and he didn't want to push his luck too far and upset the supervisor. He drove back into Salisbury to return to work, with the metal box he had uncovered sitting on the passenger seat beside him. It was so frustrating not to be able to find out what was in it immediately, but his job was important to Bill and he knew where his priorities lay. When he got back to the factory, he placed the box out of sight under the passenger seat. It would just have to stay there until he finished work and he'd need to somehow contain his impatience until then.

Back in his car at the end of the day, Bill pulled the box out from under the seat and began to study it. Despite the rust and the fact that most of the paint had flaked off, he could still make out the embossed maker's name on the lid. It said, 'William Crawford & Sons'. Bill was beside himself with joy. The man in his vision had been holding a tin of Crawford's biscuits and although its condition had seriously deteriorated, there was no doubt in Bill's mind that this was the same tin. He frantically tried to open it, but couldn't shift the lid. A closer look revealed that someone had wound black insulating tape right round where the edges of the lid fitted over the sides, completely sealing it shut. He picked away at the tape and after a couple of minutes, was able to unwind what remained of it. Taking a firm hold of the lid, he prised it open to expose a pristine interior. The insulating tape had done a good job and protected the inside of the tin from the elements. There was only a single slip of paper at the bottom of the box and his hand was shaking as he picked it up to look at it.

He hadn't known quite what to expect but recognised what it was he was holding in his hand. It was a numbered ticket from the left luggage office at Salisbury Railway Station. Someone had obviously deposited something there and then buried the ticket they'd been given in a biscuit tin at a bus stop some miles away. This was becoming crazier by the minute. The slip gave no indication as to what might have been left at the station, but there was a date on it and that date was 2nd August 1957. It was now Monday 3rd August 1964, so that meant that the ticket was seven years old.

Bill's mind went back to the vision he'd had at the bus stop and it now seemed more than likely that the past event he had somehow witnessed actually took place in August 1957, quite probably on the same day that the ticket had been issued. He'd had his dream about riding around in the Anglia Super during the early hours of Sunday morning and it was later the same day that he'd visited the bus stop and had a vision of seeing the tin being buried, and that all happened yesterday. Yesterday's date was 2nd August, so the time difference between the ticket being buried and him dreaming of riding around in the Anglia and then visiting the bus stop wasn't just approximately seven years, the two events were exactly seven years apart to the day.

Bill was very stunned by this realisation and felt that he must now be getting closer to discovering what this was all about. He had been meant to find this ticket and the Anglia in that showroom in Salisbury had somehow led him to it. What was it about that car and what had been left at Salisbury Railway Station? He had to find out and there was no time like the present.

He fairly raced to the station and for once in its life;

the old Standard Eight behaved itself and didn't play up. He parked the car and ran up the steps into the station. The left luggage office was closed for the day and wouldn't open again until eight o'clock in the morning. Bill felt more frustrated than ever. He had come so close, only to have his hopes dashed by the closed sign in the office window. He began to walk away dejectedly when a sudden noise caused him to stop and turn around. A man had just come out of the door of the luggage office and was in the act of locking it behind him.

'Excuse me,' Bill said to the man. 'I know you've closing for the night but I couldn't get here any earlier and I desperately need to retrieve something that was left here a few years ago.'

The office clerk glanced at his watch and after a few moments consideration, asked Bill if what he needed to collect was really that urgent. When Bill told him that it was, the man shrugged and put his key back in the lock. 'Okay then,' he said, 'but you'll have to be quick. I've got my dinner waiting for me when I get home.'

Bill walked into the office behind the clerk and then gave him the ticket that he had found in the biscuit tin. The man took it, checked his book and then walked off into the storeroom. He was gone several minutes and when he returned, he was dragging a big suitcase. 'There are two more of these you know,' he muttered, grumbling about the fact that he was getting too old to have to keep moving such heavy things around.

'Can I help at all,' Bill asked. 'I really do appreciate you putting in all this effort for me.'

The clerk was pleased that someone was finally showing some appreciation for all the hard work he did and led Bill into the storeroom. It was crammed full of boxes, bags and cases and they had to clamber past a number of obstacles and innumerable umbrellas to get to the very back of the room where the remaining two suitcases were sitting. 'These must have been here for a very long time,' he told Bill. 'I didn't even know they were there.'

Between them, they lugged the last two suitcases out from the storeroom and dragged them through to the office. The clerk got Bill to sign his book to say that he had taken receipt of the cases and then looking at them said, 'You're going to need a sack barrow for those mate, hang on and I'll go and get you one.'

A few minutes later, after giving the left luggage office clerk a shilling as a tip, Bill wheeled the sack barrow out of the station and towards where he had parked the Standard. He didn't know what was in the cases and couldn't wait to find out, but he knew that it had to be something special. There was no outside access to the boot on a Standard Eight, but his was a four door car and that made things easier. He opened up one of the back doors and loaded the cases straight onto the back seat. Deidre would by now be wondering what had become of him, so he knew he should head home at once, rather than try to open the cases here at the station. He had a burning curiosity to find out what was in them, but that would now have to wait until he got home. They had been in storage for the last seven years and could wait for another half an hour or so before revealing their secret.

Back in 1957, Mr X had been faced with the problem of how to deliver the suitcases to the left luggage office at the station without getting caught doing so. There was nothing extraordinary about his appearance, but the same could not be said for Joe MacNally. He stood out like a sore thumb wherever he went, so Mr X dropped him off before going to the station, after instructing Joe to stay out of sight until he returned to pick him up.

The police would by now be combing Salisbury on the lookout for the bank robbers and Mr X wasn't at all surprised to see a policeman standing guard at the railway station. His job would be to keep an eye out for any suspicious characters trying to board a train as their means of escaping the area. He parked the van in the car park and stepped out of it. A boy cycled by and Mr X hailed him.

'How would you like to earn yourself a quid?' he asked the lad.

'What would I have to do for it, mister?'

'I want you to go into the station there and bring me a sack barrow from off the platform. When you've done that, we're going to load my suitcases on it and then you will take them to the left luggage office in the station and deposit them there. They will issue you with a receipt and once you've got that ticket, you are to come straight back here and give it to me.'

'That sounds easy enough,' the boy said, 'but how can I be sure you'll pay me? You might just drive off when you've got your ticket and I'd have done all that hard work for nothing.'

Mr X warmed to the lad immediately. He was a suspicious young fellow and that was probably a good thing. 'I'll tell you what,' he said. 'I'll give you ten bob now and trust you not to ride off with it. Then, when you come back with the left luggage ticket, I will give you another thirty bob.'

'Fair enough,' said the boy, holding out his hand. He was back with the barrow in a couple of minutes and when it was loaded up with the suitcases, he started wheeling it towards the station. Mr. X had deliberately parked the van out of sight of the policeman by the entrance, but the officer did spot the lad struggling to drag his heavy load up the station steps. Mr X's heart jumped into his mouth when he began to descend the steps. He was making straight for the boy with the sack barrow and the three suitcases full of loot.

'Here, let me give you a hand with that, son,' the policeman said. 'It looks a bit heavy for a lad your size.' Together, they dragged the barrow up to the top of the steps and the policeman then went back to his post. Mr X fell about laughing. Five minutes later, he had the left luggage ticket in his hand and his young accomplice had ridden off with two pounds in his pocket. Like the rest of his plan, this stage of the proceedings had gone without a hitch and it would never occur to the forces of law and order that the money from the bank robbery was hidden right under their noses at the local railway station.

When Bill got home, he lugged the three suitcases into the house and dumped them on the floor of the lounge. Deidre was in the kitchen and yelled out, 'About time you got home!' The two boys were busy trying to open them when Bill returned from shutting the front door, but the locks were defeating them.

'You two go up and play in your room for a while,' he told them. 'What's in those suitcases has nothing to do with you.' They reluctantly obeyed but hesitated when they reached the bottom of the stairs. He ended up having to chase them up to their bedroom and shutting them in. When he returned to the lounge, Deidre was in there and was standing staring at the cases with a puzzled expression.

'What's in them?' she asked suspiciously.

'I don't know,' he said, 'but we are about to find out'. Using the screwdriver he had brought from the car, he prised open the locks on the first case and opened its lid. It was crammed full of stacks of bank notes. He quickly opened the other two cases and then stared at their contents. He couldn't believe he was seeing.

'Where did all this money come from?' Deidre almost screamed. 'You haven't robbed a bank or something like that, have you?'

'No,' said Bill, 'but I'm beginning to think that someone else might have done just that.' The way the two men at the bus stop had been acting was extremely odd to say the least, but now that he'd discovered what they'd been hiding and that it led to all this money, he was pretty sure he knew exactly what they had been up to. He could remember reading about the big bank robbery in Salisbury some years ago and although he couldn't quite recall exactly when it was, he knew it was a good six or seven years ago. If he was right, then what he had just found was the missing money from that bank job. There was far more here than he could possibly earn in his lifetime but now that he had it, what on earth was he supposed to do with it?

# 6

# HOW MUCH?

After Colin and Christopher had gone to bed, Bill tipped the contents of all three cases out onto the floor and he and Deidre started counting the money. This took them a couple of hours and by the end of that time, they were completely surrounded by comparatively neat stacks of bank notes, each containing one thousand pounds. Bill totted up the piles of notes and after adding on the amount in the smaller pile that had less than a thousand in it, he had a total.

'There is seventy-seven thousand, six hundred and ninety-four pounds here,' he told Deidre. Did you think you would ever see so much money in one place?'

She was still trying to get over the shock of what he'd discovered and didn't answer him immediately. When she managed to find her voice again, she simply said, 'It's amazing!'

He had by now explained to her how he had found the money and his story seemed even more incredible than the sight of all the stacks of bank notes sitting on their lounge carpet. 'So you are saying that the car in the showroom showed you where to look for the ticket and that you had another dream while you were standing there at the bus stop and saw those crooks burying it in a biscuit tin. That is what you just said, isn't it?'

'That is exactly what happened,' he told her. There

seems to be something magical about that car, but I can't really explain how that can be. It seems to have decided that it wants me to be its owner and led me to making this discovery. It even called out to me from across the street to get me to come and look at it.'

'There's enough money here for you to buy a fleet of cars,' Deidre commented, 'let alone that one in the showroom.'

'True,' Bill agreed, 'but that Ford Anglia Super is the one I want and it wants me as well.'

'That's freaky,' she said, 'but it doesn't get away from the fact that we are sitting here surrounded by stacks and stacks of stolen bank notes and need to decide what we are going to do about it. You're not thinking of keeping it, are you?'

The same thought had obviously been going through his mind as well, but there was no way that he could possibly do that. It was stolen money and would need to be returned to its rightful owner. 'We are going to have to call the police,' he said simply. 'They will be able to tell us what to do with it.'

'Well, I wouldn't tell them about the dreams and visions you claim to have been having,' Deidre suggested. 'They'd think you're nuts and probably cart you off somewhere.'

'I suppose you're right. I will need to think of some other way of explaining how I found that ticket.'

They didn't have a telephone in the house, so Bill went outside to use the phone box on the corner. As he stood there with the receiver in his hand and his finger poised over the dial, he realised that this would be the first time he had ever had to call '999'. 'I would like to report finding a large amount of money that I think may be stolen,' he told the officer he spoke to. 'There is quite a lot of it, so would it be possible for you to send a constable round to our house to take charge of it?'

'How much is a lot of money?' the officer at the station asked him, followed by an incredulous 'How much?' when Bill told him that it was just under seventy-eight thousand pounds.

The police car turned up at the house less than five minutes later. It contained a police inspector, a sergeant and one constable. Minutes later, all three of them were standing in Bill and Deidre's lounge staring at all the piles of bank notes on the floor. 'Exactly how and where did you find all this money, sir?' the inspector asked.

Bill had decided to pretend that he'd found the left luggage ticket in a book he had borrowed from the library for the boys. It sounded a lot more convincing than the truth and the police seemed quite happy to accept this. When asked which book it was, he showed them a copy of Robert Louis Stevenson's 'Treasure Island'. They told him they would need to keep it as evidence and Bill was happy to go along with this, providing the police agreed to pay any fine that may become due if the book wasn't returned to the library by its due date.

Having taken his statement and loaded all the notes back into the suitcases, the police then left with the cases, promising to be in touch with them again as soon as possible. Bill hadn't mentioned that he thought the money was probably connected with the bank robbery in Salisbury some years previously, but they were the police after all and he expected them to come to the same conclusion soon enough.

Deidre did ask if there was likely to be a reward for finding the money, but the inspector replied that he couldn't say at this stage of their enquiries. He did however thank them both for being honest citizens.

With all the excitement over, they both went and sat there on the sofa staring at the carpet which, until a short while ago, had been covered with thousands and thousands of pounds in bank notes. 'I suppose we did the right thing,' Bill said, 'but I now wish I'd kept back six hundred pounds so that I could afford to go and buy that Ford Anglia Super.'

'Not that car again!' Deidre said in exasperation. 'I think I've had all I can take on that subject for one day. If that magical car you seem to want so much is meant to be yours, then it will just have to work its magic again and produce some honest money with which you can pay for it. If it does that, then I'll even be happy to come along to the showroom with you to buy it.'

'That's a deal,' said Bill.

Life returned to normal for the family after that and Bill continued to go to work each day, while Deidre cleaned the house, did the shopping and prepared their meals. That was until the Friday evening, when there was a ring on the doorbell at just after seven o'clock. Bill opened the door to find a man in a suit standing there.

'My name is Albert Entwistle,' he said. 'I am the manager of the Midland Bank in Salisbury High Street and I've come to talk to you about the money you found and handed in to the police.'

Bill invited him in and led the way to the lounge. Deidre was in the middle of putting the boys to bed, but she called down from upstairs to ask him who was at the door. 'Just someone to see me,' Bill shouted back up, knowing that she'd be down the stairs like a shot, to find out for herself what was going on.

When the bank manager was comfortably seated, he produced a newspaper out of his attaché case and handed it to Bill. It was dated Saturday 3rd August 1957. 'This is an account of a robbery which took place at my bank the previous day,' he said. 'The thieves escaped with a considerable amount of money and the police were never able to apprehend them or to find any trace of the missing cash.'

'Are you suggesting that the money I found was part of the haul from that bank robbery?'

'I would go further than that,' Albert said. 'I think that what you found was the entire haul. The robbers probably didn't have enough time to divide it up between themselves and put the whole lot in those suitcases that were deposited at the railway station.'

'Wow!' said Deidre, who was now standing in the doorway.

'So, what about the crooks who took it?' Bill queried. 'You say they were never caught?'

'The police had their suspicions at the time as to who was responsible for the crime, but were never able to bring anyone to justice. One of the members of a London gang they thought was probably involved was killed a few days later and I was able to identify him as one of the armed men at the bank. He had a long scar on his face and I saw this even though he was wearing a stocking over his head at the time.'

'Was he a huge giant of a man?' Bill asked.

'How on earth did you know that?'

'Just a wild guess.' He glanced over to Deidre by the

door with an 'I told you so' expression on his face.

'The ringleader of this particular gang was never caught,' Albert went on to say, 'and to the best of my knowledge, has never been seen since that day.'

'So, what about the money?' Deidre asked. 'Is there a reward for finding it?'

'There is indeed,' Albert told her. 'The bank is prepared to pay you a finder's fee of one percent of the money recovered, which amounts to £776 18s 10d, when rounded up to the nearest penny.'

With this, he reached into his attaché case again and brought out a cheque, which he passed over to Bill. Deidre was at his side in a flash and stared at the cheque in Bill's hand. 'Bill glanced up at her and said, 'You do realise this is honest money. I trust you still remember our deal.' She could do nothing but nod her head in agreement.

After Albert had left, Bill just couldn't stop staring at the cheque. It was obviously nothing like the huge sum of money they had been looking at a few days ago, but it was more than enough to buy the Anglia and there would be plenty left to be able to afford something else, perhaps a nice holiday for the family.

'You know it's going to be Saturday tomorrow,' Bill pointed out. 'How about us driving into Salisbury and visiting that Ford dealership in the High Street?'

Deidre knew when she was beaten. She had agreed to him buying the Anglia if he could come up some honest money with which to pay for it and now he had that bank cheque for more than he needed in his hand. 'Okay,' she said. 'I will talk to Gloria next door and see if she can look after the boys for a couple of hours.'

The following morning, Charlie and the man

employed to polish the cars in the showroom were standing in front of the Anglia Super and having a discussion. 'I'll be glad when this one gets sold,' Charlie said. 'There's something very strange about it and frankly, it gives me the heebie-jeebies'.

'What do you mean?' the man asked.

Charlie went on to explain that odd things always seemed to happen whenever any prospective buyers had a look at it. 'There was this bloke the other week who seemed to be quite interested in it, but when I opened up the boot to show him how much space there was inside, the lid fell down on his head and he got really angry.'

'But there's a self-locking catch on the support strut,' the other pointed out, 'so that shouldn't happen.'

'I know,' said Charlie, 'and I'm sure I heard it click into place when I opened the boot, but the lid still came down on his head.'

'That is strange, but accidents do happen.'

'Then there was this chap who was sitting inside the car and I suggested that he turn the key and start it up.'

'What happened?'

'Nothing and that's the point. He turned the key in the ignition and nothing happened. Even the starter motor wasn't turning over.'

'Flat battery?'

'Well, I obviously thought of that but the battery was fine. The car just refused to start. After this chap had gone, I sat in it myself, turned the key and the engine fired up immediately. It was as if the car had somehow decided that it didn't like this particular customer sitting inside it and wasn't going to start for him.'

'Anything else?'

'Well, I was showing it to another customer and had the bonnet up and the engine running. He was just standing there leaning up against the wing and all of a sudden, he got a tremendous electric shock. He was literally thrown backwards and I could see he was really hurt. He lost all interest in the car after that.'

'But all these events could have a perfectly logical explanation,' the other chap pointed out.

'Yeah, well how about this one then. When the boss went round and checked the mileages on all the cars last Monday morning, the readout on this Anglia was showing thirty miles more than the delivery mileage he had in his book. He accused me of having taken it out for a joyride, but I hadn't been out in it. In fact, no one has yet gone out for a test drive in this car. All the cars have a few miles on the clock when we take delivery of them, but this Anglia's mileage has somehow increased by thirty miles. That can only mean that it's been out of the showroom and driven about without me or anyone else here knowing about it and that's impossible.'

'So what are you saying? That it went off for a drive on its own? That would suggest it's a living thing that can not only think for itself, but then do whatever it decides to do without us being involved, or perhaps you think there's some evil spirit controlling what it does!'

'I don't know what to think,' Charlie told him. 'I just want to see it out of here.'

Well you never know, someone may walk in off the street today and take it off your hands. Best of luck to you if they do, but keep your wits about you and make sure that the Anglia doesn't try to frighten off your potential buyer.'

# 7

# A DREAM COME TRUE

When Bill walked into the showroom, Charlie's face lit up. He then saw Deidre follow him in and the smile disappeared from his face. He was pleased to see Bill back, as that meant he was still interested in the Anglia, but why did he have to bring his wife along as well. At least she didn't have the two brattish kids in tow this time, so that was something of a blessing.

'Good morning, sir,' he said. 'Nice to see you again.' Turning to Deidre he forced a smile and greeted her as well. 'So you couldn't resist coming to have another look at the Ford Anglia Super, sir and I don't blame you. It's such a wonderful car that it has that effect on people.'

'You will need to convince me that it's wonderful as well,' Deidre pointed out in a no-nonsense tone, 'before we dip into our pockets and buy the thing.'

She had just said that magic word 'buy', the one that all salesmen want to hear. When someone mentions that word, they know that things have moved beyond the 'just thinking about it' stage and that they are actually considering making a purchase. Charlie was so pleased that he could have rushed over and hugged Deidre, but he wasn't brave enough to risk doing something like that. Bill wouldn't give him any problems, as he already seemed sold on the car, but he would need to tiptoe around this woman and make sure that he did everything he possibly could to convince her that the Anglia Super was the perfect car for them.

'Perhaps Madame would like to sit in the Anglia?' He suggested. 'You will find it extremely comfortable. Do you drive?'

Deidre told him that she didn't, so he opened the passenger door. He had expected some sort of argument from her, but she climbed straight in and then began looking round the inside of the car. Charlie breathed a sigh of relief and began pointing out the Anglia's internal features to her. He was amused at her startled expression when she pulled down the sun visor and saw a reflection of her own face in the vanity mirror. 'You only get a sun visor with a mirror on the passenger side with the Super model,' he told her. 'It is very handy for women to check their hair and makeup.'

Deidre gave a non-committal grunt and reached forward to open the glove box. 'Madame will see that there is a shelf underneath the dashboard as well, so there is plenty of storage space in the car.'

'Show her the heater,' Bill suggested. 'Our old Standard doesn't have one.'

Charlie pointed out all the various controls on the heater panel and while Deidre wasn't all that interested in knowing how the thing worked, she did acknowledge that having a heater would come in very handy during the cold weather. When she asked how easy it would be for the boys to get into the back, Charlie quickly ran round to the driver's side and lifted the seat to show her. 'The passenger seat you're sitting on lifts in exactly the same way, Madame,' he told her.

Deidre got out of the car and then turned back to lift

the passenger seat. 'That seems easy enough,' she said, 'but I see this car's only got the two doors. Wouldn't you miss not having back doors as well, Bill?'

'Well, if you think about it,' he replied. 'Unless the boys are in the car, I only ever use them to get stuff in and out of the boot. I wouldn't need to do that with this car as it has a separate boot.'

The trio walked around to the back of the Anglia and Charlie lifted the lid. Not wishing to risk another accident, he held onto it when he'd got it to the raised position. Deidre noticed this and queried whether it stayed up on its own. 'Of course it does, Madame.'

With great trepidation, Charlie let go of the lid. The self-locking mechanism for the strut had done what it was meant to do and the boot lid stayed up. Deidre and Bill surveyed its interior, as Charlie showed them where the spare wheel was snugly fitted into its own well at the back and then indicated the jack and wheel brace, neatly stored out of the way to one side. 'Plenty of space in there for anything you might want to take with you,' he told them. He was really pleased when he saw Deidre nodding her head in agreement.

Charlie thought things seemed to be going quite well. The boot lid had stayed up and the Anglia hadn't tried to electrocute his customers, but would it run? With his fingers crossed, he suggested that Bill take the driving seat and turn the key to start the engine. Bill did just that, after checking that the car was in neutral, and the engine fired up immediately. 'It's a lot quieter than the Standard,' Deidre commented.

'You will hardly hear the engine when you are driving,' Charlie said. 'The Ford engineers built a lot of sound proofing into this car and you will just whisper along, whenever you go anywhere for a ride in it.'

'I do like the whitewall tyres,' Deidre suddenly announced. 'Those, together with the shiny wheel trims and chromed hub caps, make the wheels look very smart.' Charlie couldn't believe what he was hearing. She had just said something complimentary about the car, without him needing to point out that particular feature. Perhaps he was finally getting somewhere with this woman after all.

'Can I suggest that we take the Super out for a test drive?' he asked. 'That will give you the opportunity to really appreciate its finer points.' He was pleasantly surprised when even Deidre agreed to this. With the trade plates in place, he suggested that Deidre should sit in the back, with Bill sitting in the passenger seat next to him. 'When we get out into the country a bit,' he said, 'we'll swop over and I will sit in the back, so that the pair of you can get a feel for what it will be like when you're out on your own in this car.'

The test drive went without a hitch, with Deidre even commenting that it was comfy and nice and roomy in the back. When Bill drove the Anglia, he considered it to be an absolute pleasure to drive. With its larger engine, he found the car to be very responsive and each gear selection was smooth and quiet, thanks to the synchromesh on all four forward gears. The weight of the steering was just how he liked it and the brakes did their job without any fuss or effort. The car behaved itself impeccably and there was no indication whatsoever that it could have a nasty side, if it didn't take to a particular prospective purchaser. 'I think it likes this guy,' Charlie thought to himself, before realising that he was being stupid. He was attributing human like qualities to what was in reality just a great big chunk of metal. The car cleaner had talked about the Anglia possibly having a mind of its own, but that was preposterous. Charlie still felt uneasy though and was very disturbed by the thought of such a possibility.

When they returned to the showroom, he asked Deidre how she had enjoyed the ride. 'It is a nice car,' she told him, 'but it costs an awful lot of money and I'm not sure that we should be spending that much on just a car.'

'But this Super is the top of the Anglia range,' he responded, 'and by paying that little bit more, you are getting a better quality car and a lot of extra features that the other models don't have.'

He waited for her to shoot him down but then she said, 'Maybe so, but it's not my decision. Bill would be the one who drives it and he will be the one who pays for it. He seemed to have set his heart on this particular car last weekend, so if he still wants it, then I suppose we will be buying it.'

The engine had been switched off by now and everyone was waiting to hear what Bill was going to say. He simply said, 'I still want this car.' Charlie was leaning against the Anglia with his arm resting lightly on the roof. As Bill spoke those five words, he could suddenly feel what could only be described as a sort of buzz, surging from the car's roof into his hand and up his arm. He jumped back in stunned surprise. It had felt a bit like a mild electric shock, but he knew it couldn't be that. It was as if the Anglia had just shown him how delighted it was that Bill had decided to become its owner. The thoughts he'd been having earlier came flooding back into his mind and he needed to sit down before he fell. His evident alarm was such that even Deidre expressed concern as to whether or not he was alright.

They had called into the Midland before visiting the showroom and deposited the cheque into Bill's account. He had asked when he would be able to draw on these funds and the cashier had told him that they were available immediately, as the cheque he had paid in was actually issued by the bank itself. As such, he now was in the position of being able to pay for the Anglia Super immediately, but Deidre wanted to do a bit of haggling first.

'I think you should throw in a year's car tax as well,' she told Charlie. 'That will save us fifteen pounds and I will want to know exactly what's covered and what's not covered under the warranty agreement. I presume you will also fill the tank up with petrol before we take it away from here?'

The last thing Charlie needed at this moment was an argument with Deidre about the overall total cost of the car, so he almost instantly agreed to everything she suggested. His arm still tingled and every time he glanced across in the direction of the Anglia Super, he could almost swear the car was watching him.

'We will send your details off to Swindon Vehicle Records Office today for the car to be registered and they will issue a log book in your name and a disc for the first year's road tax,' Charlie told them. 'Once we know what the car's registration number is going to be, we will get the number plates made up and put them on the Anglia.' He could see that Deidre was about to question something and anticipating what it would be, told her that there would be no charge for making up and fitting the number plates. Deidre seemed satisfied, so he had obviously guessed correctly. 'We should get the paperwork back from Swindon in a few day's time so if all goes well, the car should be ready for you to collect next Saturday, which will be the 15th August.'

Charlie then shook each of them by the hand and congratulated Bill on deciding to buy such a wonderful car as the Ford Anglia Super. 'It's a decision you will never regret,' he assured him, 'and I bet you just can't wait until next Saturday, when you will be able to drive away in your new purchase.' What he didn't say out loud was, 'and I can't wait until next Saturday either.' He had no intention of going anywhere near that car ever again and just wanted to see it driven away and out of his showroom.

'So what are we going to do with this car?' Deidre asked, as they were driving back towards Durrington. 'Perhaps we should have got that salesman to take it in part exchange.'

'It's not worth more than a few quid and I don't think he would have been willing to take it anyway,' Bill told her. 'Besides, I don't think you could possibly have got any more out of him than you did. You were very impressive in there with all that haggling and I think he was frightened of you.'

'He was certainly frightened of something. Did you see the expression on his face after you'd said you still wanted to buy the car? I don't think I've seen anyone look quite so terrified before.'

'Oh well, it's all over and done with now and in a week's time, we will be able to take possession of our brand new car. I will advertise the Standard Eight in the local paper for ten pounds and if we don't manage to get a buyer, then I will just have to take it to the dump.

'We've had some good times in this Standard Eight,' she continued. 'I shall be a bit sorry to see it go.'

'Yes, but think how much more fun we are going to have in the Anglia Super. We've never had a new car before and it will need to be cleaned and polished on a regular basis and maintained in tip top condition. We are going to have to look after it properly and then it will serve us well for years to come. The very last thing I'd want to see is for it to slowly deteriorate because we didn't take care of it. This old car was new once but just look at it now. I can't bear the thought of something like that happening to my Anglia. It would break my heart.'

8

# THE LABOURS OF HERCULES

The following day, being a Sunday, Bill made a start on doing something he'd been putting off tackling for years. He had made the decision to clear out the garage. The Standard Eight had never been inside the place in all the time Bill had owned it, but his new Anglia Super deserved better than that. It would have a roof over its head, so that it could be warm and comfortable. His dream car was not going to be left outside on the drive to contend with the extremes of English weather, but would spend its life safely protected from the elements within his garage. It would still need to be driven in bad weather, as that couldn't be avoided, but his intention was to make sure that it was tucked away at all other times.

Bill was a hoarder, in that he never threw anything away if there was the slightest chance that it might come in handy at some future date. The only problem with this philosophy was that when such a situation arose and he actually needed that 'something' he had deliberately not thrown away, he could never remember where he'd put it and would end up having to buy another one, usually two days before the missing item miraculously resurfaced.

The garage was his repository for such treasures and over the years, it had been progressively crammed full of all sorts of potentially useful items, plus all the things that they couldn't keep in the house. As he opened the garage's double wooden doors and surveyed its stacked interior, he didn't know where to start. It had all sounded so easy when he'd been talking to Deidre the previous evening and announced his intention of clearing out the garage, but in the cold light of day, the task he had set himself appeared Herculean.

Then there was the problem of what to do with all the stuff that was in there. It was one thing to pull everything out of the garage, but then it would need to be put somewhere else or it would have to be got rid of, which went against Bill's philosophy as a hoarder. He knew he wasn't man enough for the job facing him and that he would need to enlist Deidre's help. She was far more pragmatic when it came to deciding what to keep and what to throw away and although he knew he would probably regret asking for her assistance, he couldn't see that he had any other choice.

Back in the house, he bit the bullet and said, 'If I drag everything out of the garage, would you be prepared to sort through it and make a pile of things to keep? All the rest will have to go to the dump but I know that if I try to make that decision, we probably won't get rid of anything at all.'

'That's for sure,' she replied, 'and that's the reason why the garage is so full of your rubbish.'

'Well, you won't let me get a garden shed,' he argued. 'I've been wanting one for years.'

This was true enough, but Deidre also knew that any garden shed they bought would end up just like the garage and be full of useless items in next to no time. It was bad enough that he had crammed so much into a space that was designed to house a car and the very last thing she needed was a garden shed stuffed full of rubbish as well. She could envisage the thing bursting at the seams and disgorging all its contents onto the back lawn. 'I will help you,' she agreed, 'but I don't want to hear you whining and bellyaching when I decide what goes.'

Bill knew he would have to accept this, even if it meant him losing a few things that he considered to be potentially useful. The important thing was that the garage needed to be cleared out to provide a home for his new Anglia and if that meant making a few sacrifices, then that was the price he would have to pay. Deidre followed him out to the garage and work began.

He looked at the deckchair he had just found. One of its wooden struts had broken, but it was quite repairable and certainly something that was worth keeping. 'That's going,' Deidre said in a firm tone. Bill reluctantly handed it over to be added to the discard pile, which was growing larger by the minute. The much smaller pile of things they were keeping didn't seem to be getting any bigger at all. She was even making him throw out the Solex carburettor he'd picked up for a couple of bob at a breaker's yard a few years ago. He felt sure it would come in handy one day, but Deidre had just taken one look at it and declared that it had to go. When he questioned this, she simply told him that there was no point in keeping any old car bits when he'd just bought himself a brand new car.

As the morning progressed, Bill began to make headway through the piles of stuff in the garage until he finally reached the far wall. When he turned round to face the doors again, there was hardly anything left on the floor. He looked across at all the old tins of paint and boxes of odds and sundries that were stacked on the shelves he had put up along the side walls. There were probably some things there that were worth keeping, but Deidre had other ideas. 'How many years ago was it that you last came in here and actually used any of the things stored on those shelves?' The answer had to be several years ago and that was good enough, as far as she was concerned. 'If you haven't found a use for that stuff in umpteen years, then you certainly don't need to keep any of it now. It all goes to the dump.'

The garage was finally cleared out and Bill knew that he couldn't have done it without Deidre's help. He would need to make several trips to the dump to get rid of all the things they weren't keeping, but she had begrudgingly allowed him to hang on to a few bits and pieces and he might be able to salvage a few more from the discard pile, providing he could grab them while she wasn't looking. Deidre had however anticipated him attempting to do just that and announced that she would be coming to the dump with him to make sure that he didn't.

Christopher and Colin had been playing with the kids next door while the garage was being emptied, as Deidre didn't want them under her feet while the work was going on. Having checked with their neighbour to make sure she was happy to hang on to the boys for a while longer, she helped Bill load the car and they set off on the first of several trips to the local council dump, which was fortunately open on Sundays.

A couple of hours later, Bill stood in the doorway of the garage and stared at the open space in front of him. What few things she'd let him keep were tidily arranged on the shelves at either side and he now knew exactly what was there and where to find it. It was an amazing transformation, all thanks to Deidre taking a firm hand in deciding what had to go, and the place was now ready for when he took delivery of his shiny new car. That would be in six days time and he couldn't wait for next Saturday to arrive.

The cheque he had written out to buy the Anglia was for exactly £575. Deidre had refused to allow him to include the odd 10s 5d and Charlie wasn't prepared to argue about it. If his boss criticised this decision, then he would make up the difference himself. He would receive a tidy commission for making the sale anyway and it was a small price to pay to see the back of that Anglia Super. He had never had the same feelings before about any of the other cars he had sold, but there was something about the Anglia that really spooked him.

He knew he hadn't imagined the physical shock he had felt when the customer had said he still wanted to buy the car and that other customer had actually been electrocuted. Cars don't do that to people, but this one apparently did. And then there was the thing about the extra miles on the speedo. How could that have possibly happened if the car hadn't moved? He knew the gauge was working properly, because he had checked the mileage on it before and after taking Bill and Deidre for their test drive and it had ticked up those extra miles exactly as it should. There was definitely something very odd about that car, but the idea of it having a life and mind of its own was just too far-fetched for him to accept.

But just supposing something like that was possible. It

would challenge everything he had been brought up to believe. But there again, he would never have believed that spaceflight was possible, until the Russians proved him wrong three years previously by sending Yuri Gagarin up in a rocket to orbit the Earth. There was no doubt that science fiction was fast becoming science fact, but a car that could think for itself and display emotions? Even the science fiction and comic book writers hadn't come up with an idea quite as daft as that yet.

The car Charlie was thinking about was sitting minding its own business in the showroom in Salisbury. Car dealerships didn't open on a Sunday, so the place was unlit and deserted. It would be twenty years before the film 'Terminator' suggested the idea of machines becoming self-aware and the machines that did were all highly computerised to begin with. There were no computerised elements or parts fitted to the Ford Anglia, as it was of an age before cars incorporated any such complex electronics.

The spark of life that made the engine run was basically generated mechanically. The battery provided the power to the coil and this transformed it from twelve to something in the order of twenty thousand volts, with a capacitor being used to store this on a temporary basis. A contact breaker formed part of the distributor, which was mechanically driven from the camshaft, and fed this high voltage to the spark plugs in the appropriate firing order, as predetermined by the crankshaft which moved the pistons. When this power reached the end of each plug, it jumped the gap between the central and ground electrodes and in doing so, created the spark required to ignite the petrol air mixture in the cylinders. It was a fairly simple arrangement and comparatively foolproof, so there was no reason why the car should refuse to want to start one minute, but then be quite happy to work perfectly just a few minutes later.

All the rest of the car's electrics were equally uncomplicated. The wiring loom connected the battery to all the fitted electrical equipment by means of switches inside the car and the mechanically driven dynamo kept the battery fully charged. There was nothing there to suggest that a life force could possibly be created electrically, or within the ignition system, and the rest of the car was constructed out of metal, glass, plastic and rubber. It just didn't seem credible that it could actually have become self-aware and have a mind of its own but as Charlie had said, there was definitely something odd about it. It seemed to be making a habit of doing things one wouldn't expect from any normal car and this was why this particular Ford Anglia Super scared Charlie witless.

# 9

# THE WAITING GAME

The week dragged by interminably for Bill. He got up each day, went to work, came home, had his dinner and then went to bed. All he could think about was that he would be taking possession of his new Ford Anglia Super on the Saturday and that day couldn't come soon enough for him. He tried to take his mind off the slow passage of time by planning a holiday for the family. He still had around £200 left from the reward money and that was far more than he would need to take the family on a really special holiday.

The boys wouldn't be back at school for another three weeks and with the holiday season now coming to an end, there were bound to be some last minute bookings available at very reasonable prices. It wasn't that Bill was stingy when it came to spending money, but he did like to keep an eye out for any bargains that might come along.

The factory where he worked had been closed for a week in early July for all its employees to take their annual holiday, but Christopher had been getting over mumps at the time, so the family had not been able to go away. Had they done so, then Bill would have probably booked a caravan by the seaside for them, but that wasn't what he had in mind for this holiday. With the English weather being what it is, there was always the possibility of a few days rain, irrespective of when they went, and he didn't like the idea of his new Anglia having to sit out in a muddy field, while the family could do no more than watch the rain through their caravan windows. He didn't want to risk that happening, so a caravan holiday was definitely out.

Many people were now taking advantage of the cheaper air flights available to holiday destinations on the continent, but it would be no good Bill considering anywhere abroad, as he didn't have a passport and neither did Deidre.

He had once taken them all to Butlins for a week, but their chalet there was very basic and the entire holiday was far too regimented. It reminded Bill of his time in the army, with the barrack like accommodation blocks and everyone having to eat their daily meals together at a set time. Everyone even had to display the badges they'd all been given, or they wouldn't be allowed back into the camp after visiting the beach. Turning up late for meals invariably meant that most of the food had gone, and whilst the boys had thoroughly enjoyed all the entertainment laid on for kids, going to a holiday camp was not the sort of experience Bill particularly wanted to repeat in a hurry.

No, this holiday had to be something special, a once in a lifetime opportunity that they probably wouldn't be able to afford to do again. But what to do and where to go? In future times, planning a special holiday would become quite a simple task because of the internet, but that didn't exist in 1964 and as Bill didn't even have a phone in the house; it would mean him having to go to see a travel agent, which he could only do during his lunch break. He knew he wouldn't have any problems getting a week off work, as he still had another nine days holiday due to him. There was also the point that his bosses knew the family hadn't been able to go away on holiday in July because of Christopher and his mumps, so they wouldn't mind too much that he would only be giving them short notice.

It was now the Thursday evening, still another thirty-seven hours to go before he could collect his Anglia, so he broached the subject with Deidre. 'I want to spend some of the rest of the reward money on a special holiday for us all. I was thinking about doing this before the boys have to go back to school, so can you think of anywhere special that you would like to go?'

'I haven't really thought about it,' she said. 'I'm sure there must be better ways to use that money than to spend it on a holiday.'

'But this one is to be a really special holiday,' he told her. 'Getting given that money was a stroke of luck and it enabled me to buy the car of my dreams. I want the rest of the family to be able to share in my good fortune by going somewhere and doing something that we wouldn't normally be able to afford.

'Well, if you put it that way, I would love to go somewhere nice, but we all have our dreams you know.'

Bill mentally kicked himself for not thinking of this earlier. He wasn't the only one in the family to dream of buying something he couldn't afford. Deidre had been really taken with an expensive dress she'd seen on their shopping trip to Salisbury the other week, but didn't buy it because she couldn't justify spending that much money on just a dress. Colin and Christopher had been going on for ages about him buying them a Hornby

Dublo train set, but they were quite expensive and he hadn't had enough spare money available to make their dream come true.

'I tell you what,' he said. 'When we go into Salisbury to collect the Anglia on Saturday, we will stop off at the dress shop to buy that frock you liked so much. It will be just the thing for you to wear when we go on our holiday. We will also call into the big toy shop in the High Street and buy a top of the range train set for the boys. They will be absolutely thrilled when they see it. That way, everyone gets something they've dreamed of and it won't even make much of a dent in the £200 I've got.'

Deidre gave him a great big hug. 'That would be wonderful,' she said. 'I really would love to have that dress and a train set would keep the boys engrossed in their room for hours on end and give us a bit of peace. As for the holiday, if the cost really doesn't matter, then I'm sure we'll be able to come up with something the whole family will enjoy. I will need to think about it for a while but you can cross Butlins off the list as I don't want to go back there. That place was too much like a prison camp with the redcoats as guards.'

Saturday finally arrived and after leaving the boys with Gloria next door, Bill and Deidre set off to Salisbury on the bus. He would have taken the Standard but for the fact that Deidre couldn't drive. With two cars and only one driver, this would have left him with the problem of how to get their old car back to Durrington. He had placed an advert for the Standard in the local newsagent's shop earlier in the week, but no one had expressed any interest in it so far.

Although he was desperate to get to the car dealership

to take possession of his beloved Anglia Super, Bill decided to get the shopping part of the trip over and done with first and to buy Deidre her posh dress and the train set for the boys. These could go into the boot of the Anglia and then there would be nothing else to delay the main event, which would be that magical moment when he could take the wheel of his dream car and drive it for the first time as its new owner. That would be special and he didn't want to spoil the experience by only driving the Anglia from the showroom to a car park and then having to go and do shopping. It probably would have been sensible for the pair of them to visit one or two travel agents while they were in Salisbury, but that would inevitably have taken some time and he didn't want to put off his magical moment for any longer than was absolutely necessary. There was a limit to his patience and he'd had to wait a whole week already.

At the dress shop, Deidre insisted on trying the dress on to make sure it fitted properly. 'Of course it will,' he told her. 'That dress is a size 12 and you always buy that size. Is it really worth bothering when you know it will fit?'

'I'm still going to try it on just to make sure,' she said, before walking off to the changing room with the dress over her arm. Bill glanced at his watch for the tenth time in the last five minutes. This was taking forever. The saleslady was busy laying other items on the counter and Bill realised in horror that she was setting out matching accessories for Deidre to look at. He glanced at his watch again.

'How long does it take to try a dress on?' he asked himself about five minutes later. Still no sign of Deidre.

She finally came out of the changing room wearing the dress. She hadn't even changed back into what she had been wearing. This really was going to take forever. He looked down at his watch again.

'Do you like it?' Deidre asked, as she paraded in front of a full length mirror.

'It's lovely,' he said. 'Now take it off, get it wrapped and then we can get out of here.'

She started walking back towards the changing room but then noticed the other items the saleslady had laid out. Changing course, she headed straight for the counter and began looking at the things there. 'These shoes would go well with this dress,' she said, holding them up. 'What do you think Bill?'

It was at about this point that he wished he hadn't given up smoking two years previously. He felt that he could really do with a cigarette right now. 'I'll tell you what,' he suggested in desperation. 'I will go to the toy shop and buy that train set and then come back here. You can get anything you want and I will pay for it. This is your special treat, so I don't mind what you buy as long as you like it.'

The saleslady heard that magic word 'buy' and promptly rushed off to find some more items for Deidre to look at. This was the final straw for Bill and he ran out of the shop as fast as he could.

He didn't think it would take him long to select a train set for the boys as he knew they would be delighted with whichever one he bought them. What he didn't take into account however was the fact that a Saturday morning during school holidays is possibly the worst time to visit a toy shop. The place was heaving with kids and parents and there was only one harassed salesman trying to deal with all of them. He joined the long queue for the counter and checked his watch again.

In the car showroom, Charlie was also looking at his watch. He had expected Bill to be standing outside when the doors opened, but it was already ten-thirty and there was still no sign of him. 'I wonder what's keeping him,' he asked himself.

By the time Bill finally reached the counter it was nearly eleven o'clock. 'I want to see some train sets,' he told the salesman.

'And you've come to the right place,' the man said. 'Now would that be a Hornby Dublo set or a Triang one? We stock both and have a wide variety from which you could make your choice. Will your children want a steam locomotive or a diesel one and will they want passenger carriages or goods wagons?'

'Hornby, steam, passenger carriages, plus a tender for the locomotive.' Bill listed off for him.

'And would that be for our local Great Western line, or for one of the other regional networks?'

'Great Western,' Bill replied.

'Very good, sir. Now what about the track layout? What sort of size are you thinking of and would you be wanting points, buffers, sidings, a turntable and possibly a level crossing?'

'I just want a train set.' Bill told him in exasperation. 'Show me the most expensive one you've got and I will buy it.'

The salesman walked off to the storeroom with a delighted expression on his face. Not only had Bill said the magic 'buy' word but he had also said that he wanted to see the most expensive train set in the shop. Now this was the type of customer he really liked.

It was a good five minutes before he returned carrying an enormous box, which he plonked onto the counter.

Bill was taken aback at its size and wondered whether the Anglia's boot would be big enough to accommodate it. The salesman removed the lid with some difficulty and then stepped back to allow Bill to view the contents. It was crammed full of pieces of track in various shapes and sizes and most importantly, a magnificent steam locomotive in the livery of the Great Western Railway, complete with its own tender. There were six coaches it total, all in the same livery, and a guard's box to go on the end of the train. It certainly looked impressive.

'Okay, I'll take it.'

'But I haven't told you the price yet, sir'

'Just wrap it up and I will give you a cheque.' As soon as he said this, Bill realised his mistake. It would take the man forever to wrap a box this size and he couldn't wait. He desperately wanted to get to that car showroom. 'Forget that,' he said. 'I will take it as it is.'

He fought his way out of the shop with his huge purchase and because the box was so awkward to carry, bumped into several other pedestrians on his way back to the dress shop. When he got there, he found Deidre waiting patiently in a chair. Several large shopping bags surrounded her. He walked over to the counter with his cheque book, after having left the train set with Deidre, and asked how much the bill was. She had obviously taken him at his word when he'd told her she could buy anything she liked.

At eleven thirty-five they finally entered the car showroom, both struggling under the weight of their purchases. The Ford Anglia Super was there waiting for him and now displayed '341 CHR' as its registration number. A tax disc had been affixed to the inside of its windscreen. Charlie got up from his desk and invited them to sit down opposite him, an invitation they were only too glad to accept. It didn't take long to complete the formalities and by the time these were over, Bill held in his hand the log book, his owners manual and two sets of keys for the car.

'That's it then,' said Charlie. 'Your Anglia is full of petrol and you're all set to go. I will help you load your shopping and then you can get on your way.'

The boxed train set was inevitably too large to fit into the boot and proved quite difficult to get it into the car at all. It necessitated both Bill and Charlie manhandling it through the passenger door and they could only leave it standing on the backseat obscuring rearward visibility. 'At least you've got the two wing mirrors,' Charlie said with a smile. 'Perhaps you should have asked the shop to deliver the train set for you. They've probably got a van.'

Bill was not amused, but this was going to be his magic moment and even a facetious salesman was not going to spoil it. With Deidre's shopping safely stored in the boot and her settled in the passenger seat, he got himself comfortable in the driver's seat and then turned the key to start the Anglia. Charlie had already opened the glass showroom doors and as the engine fired into life, he engaged first gear and began to drive out of the showroom.

Charlie waved and wished them 'Good luck' and then under his breath said, 'With that car you might need it!'

# 10

# LIVING THE DREAM

As he drove along the High Street, Bill was pleased to see so many pedestrians staring in admiration as he passed by. Not that many people could afford to buy a brand new car in the sixties and the sight of one driving along was therefore something of a novelty. Most of the cars on the road were getting on a bit in age and many were just as bad as his old Standard Eight. That car was coming up to its tenth birthday and would need another MOT test shortly. The MOT test had been introduced four years earlier and initially only applied to vehicles that were ten years old, and annually thereafter, but this had been reduced to seven years the following year, because of the high failure rate. As such, this would be the Standard's third MOT test and that was always a worrying time. Although the test then was nothing like as stringent as MOT tests are today, this compulsory testing of older vehicles would gradually lead to many old bangers being scrapped and a general reduction in the number of them still on the road.

One of the reasons why so few people bought new cars in the sixties was the cost in relation to their earnings. At this time, Bill was being paid £22 10s 0d a week, £1,170 per annum, and the basic rate of income tax in 1964 was 38.75%. Having a wife meant that he benefited from an increased personal tax allowance and there was also the weekly family allowance paid because they had two children, but the family's net income wasn't great and didn't stretch all that far.

New cars were also considered to be 'luxury goods' and as such were subject to purchase tax, which was 25% in 1964. In the case of Bill's Anglia, the actual price he paid was £575, of which £115 was purchase tax. It is clear to see that buying a new car in the sixties represented a considerable investment and there was also the point that it would begin to depreciate in value the moment you drove it out of the showroom.

It is little wonder that not that many people bought new cars at this time and Bill would never have been able to afford his new Ford Anglia Super, but for the reward money paid for discovering Mr X's hidden loot.

As purchase tax wasn't chargeable on second hand cars, many people took advantage of this fact and opted to buy a car that was just a year or two old. By then, the cost would be considerably less than that of a new car, with its inclusive purchase tax, but as far as condition went, such cars were almost new, many with just a few thousand miles on the clock. You wouldn't get the kudos of owning a brand new car but for considerably less outlay, would be in the same position as someone who had bought their car new and then kept it for a couple of years.

Bill decided to drive home using the A360, so that he could have another look at that bus stop. He stopped next to it and got out of the car. 'What are you doing now?' Deidre asked. 'Are you hoping to find another pot of gold?'

'No, it's not that,' he told her. 'I just want to stand inside that bus shelter again.'

He walked over to where the hole had been and brushed his foot across the ground where he had attempted to smooth it over after filling in the hole he'd dug. It still looked as if the area had been disturbed, but not enough to attract too much attention. Bill then went and stood inside the bus shelter. He didn't really expect to get another vision and so it came as no surprise to him when nothing happened. This place had become a turning point in his life, but there didn't seem to be anything mystical about it now. He was still very puzzled as to how the Anglia had seemed to know the significance of this location and decided to lead him to it, but that had all taken place in a dream and who really understood what dreams were all about anyway. It was still very odd though, but he clearly wasn't going to get any nearer to understanding what any of it actually meant by standing here. He began walking back to his new car.

As he started to drive off, his foot somehow slipped from the clutch pedal and the Anglia leapt forward. It began to kangaroo down the road like the cars driven by learner drivers who have yet to master the technique of clutch control. It bounced a few times before it settled down and then drove smoothly.

'Sorry about that,' he said. 'I'm not sure quite what happened there. I must be getting careless in my old age.'

She was sitting there with an odd expression on her face. 'If I didn't know better,' she told him, 'I would swear that this car just jumped for joy to show how pleased it is that you bought it!'

That made Bill stop and think for a moment. The last time he'd done something like that was donkey's years ago and there was no reason why his foot should have slipped off the clutch pedal.

When they arrived back at Durrington, Colin and Christopher came running out of the neighbour's house even before Bill had put the handbrake on. They had been staring out of the window in the front room for over an hour, expectantly awaiting the return of their parents with the family's new car. They had not been paying too much attention to the Anglia Super in the showroom, as they were far more interested in the lollypops the salesman had given them, but now they stood in awe at the sight of this shiny new car, with all its bright chrome work and go faster stripes along each side.

'Wow!' said Christopher, the first to find his voice. 'It's smashing!'

Both boys walked around the Anglia wondering whether they dare touch it. It was at this point that Colin spotted the huge box on the back seat and they both peered in through the windows to try to see what it was. 'It's a train set,' Colin suddenly yelled out. 'Daddy's bought us a train set.'

There was no settling them down after that and they were jumping up and down in excitement as Bill dragged the box out of the car and took it into the house. 'We will assemble it later,' he told the boys. 'You can have a look at it, but just don't break anything.' That would keep them occupied for a while, so he went outside again to admire his new pride and joy.

Several neighbours had appeared on the scene by now, including Gloria's husband John from next door. They were all appreciative of the Anglia's fine lines and it was pretty obvious that they were all jealous that Bill had been able to buy himself a brand new car. ‘She’s a beauty,’ John commented, ‘and I really do like the colour scheme and those whitewall tyres. ‘Is this the Anglia with the bigger engine in it?’

‘Yes,’ Bill told him. ‘It’s got the 1198 cc engine fitted and because it’s the Super model, there are a whole load of other extras on it as well, including a heater and windscreen washers as standard.’

There were quite a few gasps of admiration as Bill gave the neighbours a guided tour and showed them all the finer points of his new Anglia Super. The street party lasted for best part of half an hour, before the last of the neighbour left and Bill was finally able to go back indoors.

Colin and Christopher were sitting on the carpet and it looked as if they had taken every single piece of the train set out of the box and were busy examining each one of them in turn. ‘Aren’t you going to put your new car into the garage?’ Deidre queried. ‘You wouldn’t want something to happen to it while it’s sitting there on the drive.’

‘I will in a while,’ he told her, ‘but I just want to be able to glance at it through the window from time to time. I’m finding it hard to believe it’s now mine and that this is not just another dream. I keep pinching myself to make sure I’m awake and that it’s actually there.’

‘Well,’ she replied. ‘It’s definitely there and so is this train set you bought the boys. They are really excited about it, so don’t you think it’s time that you paid some attention to them for a while, rather than that car, and helped them put their train set together?’

'Yes, you're right of course. Come on you two, let's get all the pieces back in the box and we will take it upstairs and assemble it in the spare room. I don't think there will be enough space for a railway the size of this one in your bedroom.'

The next day, Bill took the whole family out in the Anglia. It was the first time that Colin or Christopher had been in a new car and they couldn't get over how different it was to the old Standard. The thing they loved the most however was the characteristic smell that only comes with a brand new car. They were rather puzzled that this one only seemed to have two doors, as they thought all cars had four, but they would soon get used to that and actually enjoyed the novelty of climbing into the back seat through the front doors. Bill didn't go very far on this first family outing in the Anglia, as the weather was beginning to look a bit threatening and he didn't want to risk it getting wet.

Deidre surprised him by suddenly announcing that she wouldn't mind learning how to drive. 'I wouldn't have wanted to in the old Standard,' she said, 'but this car is modern and that would make it a lot easier for me.' Bill wasn't at all sure he fancied the idea of a learner driver being let loose in his new pride and joy, but there would be some definite advantages to Deidre knowing how to drive.

'That might not be a bad idea,' he told her. 'Perhaps I should book up some lessons for you with a driving school.'

'Couldn't you teach me in the Anglia? That way we wouldn't need to spend money on lessons.'

'I'm not sure I would make a good teacher,' he said. 'Those blokes in the driving schools are professionals and know exactly what they're doing. I'd probably tell you all the wrong things.' He didn't bother to mention that driving school cars also had dual controls, whereas his beloved Anglia didn't. The idea of Deidre being at the wheel and him not having a brake pedal in front of him filled him with horror.

'You're just frightened that I might damage your new car, aren't you?'

'To be absolutely honest,' he replied, 'yes!'

'But if I was to take lessons with a school and passed my test, I presume you would let me drive it then?'

'Of course I would,' he said. The thought going through his mind was that he hoped the day she did get to drive his Anglia would be a long time coming.

When they got home, he walked slowly round the car, just to make sure it was still perfect. A few flies had splattered themselves against the windscreen but other than that, there wasn't a single blemish. He carefully cleaned off the windscreen before tucking his dream machine away in the garage.

That night, two of the local yobbos, who had walked by when Bill had been showing off his new car to the neighbours the day before, stealthily approached the garage. Their plan was to take the Anglia out for a drive and have a bit of fun in it. Neither of them had driving licenses but this didn't bother them. They would obviously be breaking the law by stealing the car anyway, so the fact that they couldn't legally drive wasn't going to make any difference.

They were not experienced car thieves with the skill necessary to pick locks, but the crowbar one of them carried would make short work of the new padlock Bill had just fitted to the garage doors and once inside, they would use it to gain entry to the car by breaking one of its windows. Hot-wiring the car's ignition circuit was something they both knew how to do and if all went according to plan; they would be away in the Anglia before anyone even knew they were there.

Success therefore only depended on them working quickly and quietly and, just as importantly, not being seen. They had stolen a number of cars for joyrides in the past and had so far got away with it every time. They had no reason to suspect that taking this car was going to be any different and they were both looking forward to the fun they'd have driving around in a brand new Ford Anglia Super. They were not hardened criminals like Mr X or Joe MacNally, but they knew what they were doing and were full of confidence.

As the one with the crowbar was working out just where to jam it in order to prise off the hasp secured by Bill's new padlock, a car horn suddenly blared out, shattering the peace and quiet of the neighbourhood. It sounded like it was coming from inside the garage and it kept sounding off every couple of seconds. The lad with the crowbar thought he had somehow set off the car's alarm. In his panic, he grabbed hold of his mate's arm and yelled, 'Let's get out of here!' The pair of them then ran off and all was peaceful again.

The odd thing about this is that Ford Anglia Supers didn't come with a fitted alarm system, but perhaps this car didn't want these young villains to take it for a joyride.

# 11

# GOING ON HOLIDAY

Bill took his shiny new car to work on Monday morning and all his workmates gathered around to have a look as soon as he arrived. They had been hearing endlessly about him getting his new Anglia for the whole of the previous week, so it didn't come as that much of a surprise to them when he turned up in it. He stepped out from the car and then stood there staring at it, an expression of sheer delight on his face.

'So you got it then?' Harry said, 'and you're clearly pleased with it.'

'This Anglia is absolutely amazing,' Bill told him. 'Being its owner is like a dream come true for me. I feel like all my birthdays have just come at once.'

'Lucky you,' Harry commented, 'and now you're a celebrity as well, from what I read in the local paper, although it doesn't actually name you.' He handed his copy of the weekly paper over to Bill.

The headline on the front page declared, 'Treasure Island Reveals Lost Fortune' and went on to explain how a local man had found the missing money from the Salisbury bank robbery in 1957, by discovering a clue to its location in the pages of a library book. They hadn't interviewed him, as the police and bank had not disclosed his name and address, but the reporters had talked to the clerk at the left luggage office at Salisbury

Railway Station. He was quoted as saying, 'Three great big suitcases there were and I helped him lug them out and even went and got him a sack barrow. If only I'd known what was in them. All I got for my trouble was a shilling as a tip and he got all the reward money. That's not fair if you ask me.'

Bill chuckled when he read the last bit. Had he known what was in the suitcases at the time, he probably would have given the clerk a bit more, but he didn't know what he'd actually found until later on.

He had agreed to meet up with Deidre at lunchtime, so that they could visit the travel agents. She would come in by bus, having left the boys with Gloria again, to see what was available in terms of a special holiday for the family. Bill made a point of checking with his bosses, to make sure they wouldn't mind him taking a week off at short notice and as anticipated, they didn't have any problem with this.

'So where would you go for a holiday if money was no object?' Bill asked the man in the travel agents.

'I'd fly to Spain and spend my time sunbathing on the beach with a jug of sangria by my side. Endless days of sunshine and fish and chips every other evening. What more could you ask for?' British holidaymakers going abroad in the sixties went principally for the sunshine and weren't yet adventurous enough to risk trying much of the local cuisine.

'No passports,' Bill told him, 'so it will have to be somewhere in this country.'

'Well, in that case,' the man suggested. 'How about a luxury seaside hotel? Some of the bigger ones have their own heated indoor swimming pools these days.'

'That would be nice,' Deidre agreed. 'We could teach

the boys how to swim. What sort of room could we get and what sort of facilities would a hotel like that have?'

'If money really is no object,' he said, 'then I would go for a suite with a sea view. You could get a two bedroomed one, so your children will have their own room to sleep in, and the hotel restaurant will serve up the finest food you're ever likely to taste. There will be porters to carry your luggage and your room will be cleaned on a daily basis, including making up the beds. Such a hotel will cater for anything and everything you might want and you wouldn't even need to lift a finger while you're there. All you would have to do is to sit back and enjoy yourselves.'

'I like the sound of that,' Bill said. 'What about parking? I wouldn't want to leave my car outside if the weather turns nasty.'

'We can't promise you perfect weather in this country, sir,' the man observed, 'but I'm sure I can find you a hotel with indoor car parking.'

'Perfect,' Bill commented. 'So can we leave it with you to find a suitable place? We're thinking of going next week.'

'I'm sure that won't be a problem, sir,' he replied. 'I will get on it straightaway and send you all the details in the post. Is there any particular part of the country where you would like to go?'

'How about the west country?' Deidre suggested. 'Somewhere in Devon or Cornwall perhaps.'

'Fine,' the man said. 'You can expect to hear from me within a couple of days and if you are happy with the place I pick for you, then just let me know and I will attend to all the arrangements. You will just need to drive there and start having a wonderful time.'

With that attended to, Bill needed to return to work. He didn't want to start making a habit of being late back from his lunch breaks.

The travel agent was as good as his word and a large envelope dropped through their letterbox on the Wednesday morning. Bill had already left for work, so wouldn't see it until that evening, but Deidre had no intention of waiting all day to see what they'd been sent. She tore the envelope open and sat down on the sofa to read its contents. The selected hotel was a four star establishment on the seafront at Paignton and had both indoor and outdoor swimming pools, as well as an underground car par. Their suite would be on the top floor, with magnificent views across the bay, and they wouldn't need to use the stairs to get there, as there were two lifts. All the pictures made the hotel look absolutely fantastic and the resort itself had a big sandy beach, a pier, and plenty of local places offering family entertainment, including a zoo full of wild animals for the boys to see. It seemed to be just about perfect to Deidre, but Bill would need to make the final decision, as it was his money they'd be spending. She couldn't wait for him to get home.

Bill was just as enthusiastic about the resort and the hotel the travel agent had selected for them as Deidre had been and he really did like the idea of his beloved Anglia being kept under cover. 'Well, if you're happy with this place,' he told Deidre, 'then I suggest we go for it. I can't see anything at all wrong with it and think we could all have a really wonderful time there.'

'I love it,' she said simply. 'I will telephone the travel agent tomorrow morning and tell him to set it all up for us. How far is it from here to Paignton?'

'It's not much more than a hundred miles, so it will probably take about three hours to get there, depending on what the traffic is like on the Exeter by-pass.'

'That's not too bad,' she said. 'If we leave straight after breakfast on Sunday, we should be there in time for Sunday lunch. Then we'll have a full week of being pampered before needing to return home the following weekend. That gives me three whole days to organise what we're going to need to take with us and to make a start on the packing.'

'Make sure you don't forget to include our swimming costumes! I hope mine still fits. I wish you hadn't made me throw out that deckchair I had in the garage. I could have fixed that and it would have come in handy for sitting on the beach.'

'We will just do what we normally do,' she told him. 'Hire some deckchairs from the beach attendant. We don't want to be carting around deckchairs all the time.'

Colin and Christopher got really excited when told about the family's planned seaside holiday and just wouldn't stop going on about it. Sunday finally arrived and while Deidre washed up the breakfast dishes, Bill loaded all the suitcases into the Anglia's boot. He was pleasantly surprised to find that they all fitted in without any difficulty, which meant that the boys wouldn't have to sit in the back of the car with one of the suitcases on their laps. This had proved necessary on quite a few occasions with the Standard. When everything and everybody was ready to go, Bill got Colin and Christopher settled on the back seat and gave them each a comic to read. The 'Eagle' for Colin and the 'Beano' for Christopher. The comics would help keep them quiet for a while, but it wouldn't be long before he could expect to hear them repeatedly asking, 'Are we there yet?' and it could get very tedious having to keep telling them that they weren't quite there yet.

The traffic was fairly light, being a Sunday morning, and their journey was virtually incident free until they began to near Exeter. The one incident that did happen was on the A303. Bill suddenly saw an Anglia like his approaching in the opposite direction and its driver was flashing his lights. He was initially confused, but then realised what was happening. They were both driving Ford Anglias and the other driver was acknowledging a fellow owner. Bill flashed his lights to return the gesture and waved enthusiastically as both cars passed each other. This had never happened to him while driving the Standard Eight, but he was now the owner of a Ford Anglia Super and as such, he had become a member of an elite club.

The Exeter by-pass in the sixties was legendary for its long traffic jams and snarl-ups and it was not unusual to end up sitting in a stationary line of vehicles for hours on end. There was no way to avoid this other than by going through the city itself, but the many drivers who tried this then found themselves getting stuck in the High Street and other narrow roads, that couldn't handle the volume of traffic attempting to drive through them. The by-pass was therefore the preferred route, despite the inevitable delays, and many families would get out of their cars and have a picnic by the side of the road, while they waited for the traffic to start moving again. The building of the M5 finally eased this problem to a certain extent, but that motorway can now rival the old by-pass in terms lengthy tailbacks, simply because there is too much traffic trying to use it, particularly during the busy summer holiday season.

Bill and his family ended up getting stuck for nearly two hours trying to get past Exeter. The boys got bored stiff and began squabbling with each other and Deidre needed to threaten to smack them if they didn't shut up. Playing 'I spy' kept them amused for a short while, but as there was not a lot to see in a traffic jam, it began to get repetitive.

When Christopher announced, 'I spy with my little eye something beginning with C,' for the fifth time, everybody began to get annoyed with him.

'It's cars again, isn't it?' Colin shouted angrily. 'You can't keep using the same word.'

'Perhaps he was thinking of C for clouds this time,' Bill suggested.

'No, I was thinking of C for cars, but there's not much else to see.'

'I don't want to play this game with him anymore,' Colin said stroppily. 'He doesn't know the rules.'

'Quiet, the pair of you,' Deidre said in a raised voice. 'If you can't play happily together then I will get your dad to turn this car around and we will all go home.' This quietened them down for a bit, but the pressure of sitting in a hot car and not moving anywhere was beginning to tell on everyone. An Anglia Super might have had a heater fitted as standard, but it didn't have air-conditioning.

Finally clear of Exeter, they only had twenty or so miles to go to reach Paignton and this was when the boys began to get really excited. They started jumping up and down on the back seat, as each of them wanted to be the first one to spot the sea. Unfortunately for them, while the A380 follows the line of the coast, it does so at a distance of four miles, so there would be no chance of them actually seeing it until they reached their destination.

'I need a wee-wee!' Christopher suddenly announced, a short while later.

'Can't you can hang on for a just few more minutes?' Deidre suggested to him. 'We're very nearly there.'

'No I can't!' he told his mum. 'I need to go right now or I'm going to wet myself.'

'You do that in my new car and you'll get the hiding of your life,' Bill shouted out. Christopher immediately burst into tears..

Crisis was however averted as they were now arriving in Paignton and just a stone's throw from the hotel. As Bill pulled up outside, Deidre leapt out and after tipping her seat forward, grabbed hold of her desperate son and yanked him from the car. With Christopher in tow, she then ran straight past the uniformed doorman on the steps and into the hotel to find the toilets. Bill just sat there for a moment to recover. It had not been the most pleasant of journeys and it had taken them nearly five hours. Not that he had any criticism of the Anglia though, as it had performed perfectly. But they were here now and about to start their holiday. Things could only get better from now on.

## 12

## CATASTROPHE IN PAIGNTON

When Deidre came out of the hotel with Christopher, she found Bill standing by the car with Colin. He was having a chat with the doorman.

'Yes,' he said. 'This is the latest Ford Anglia Super model, with the bigger engine and a whole host of extra features.'

'It is very impressive, sir. I've never seen one before and I do like the colour scheme.'

'I'm very pleased with it,' Bill told him. 'I only got it last weekend, so this is the first long journey I've done in it. It gives a very comfortable ride and there's plenty of room for all the family and our luggage.'

'Yes sir,' replied the doorman. 'I will get the porter to attend to your luggage and you can then drive round to our garage at the back of the hotel. There is a lift there that will bring you back to reception for you to sign in and then someone will take you and your family up to your room.'

'We have booked the top floor suite.'

'That's an excellent choice, sir. It is the best room in the hotel, with wonderful views of the beach and across the bay.'

The doorman summoned a porter and he led the way into the hotel. Bill let him carry their luggage. 'If you stay here with the boys,' he told Deidre, 'I will just drive the car round to the hotel garage and park it.'

Following the directions given to him by the doorman, Bill drove round to the back of the hotel. There were some workmen there digging a hole in the road right next to the entrance, which was a sloped ramp leading down to the hotel's underground car park. He swung out to pass the obstruction they were causing and then descended the ramp. The car park wasn't all that big, but it was spacious enough and he had no problem finding a place in which to park. He glanced around after he had got out of the car and was pleased with what he saw. 'Yes, I think the Anglia is going to be nice and comfortable in here.'

After ascending in the lift to the reception area, he completed the required formalities there and the family were then led up to their suite. Colin and Christopher had never been in a lift before and really loved the novel experience of riding in one. They wanted to press all the different buttons to see what they did, but Deidre firmly told them not to touch any of them.

The suite was everything they could have hoped for and the boys were delighted to discover that they had their own bedroom. A set of French doors led out to a small balcony overlooking the beach and there were several large armchairs in the room, as well as a writing desk and an occasional table. The room looked elegant, if a little on the posh side, but it most certainly looked comfortable and was definitely the most luxurious accommodation they would ever have stayed in. There was a huge double bed in the master bedroom, together with a dressing table, a full length mirror, two wardrobes and a chest of drawers. The only thing that was missing was an en-suite bathroom, but very few hotels had such facilities in the nineteen-sixties.

The porter had by now arrived with their luggage, which he took into their bedroom. 'Does the suite meet with your approval?' the lady who had brought them up from reception asked.

'It's perfect,' Deidre told her, 'and I know we are all going to be very happy here.'

They had missed Sunday lunch by a long time, but the lady told them that this wouldn't be a problem. She would arrange for some sandwiches and refreshments to be brought up to the suite. 'The restaurant will be open again at six o'clock,' she said, 'and there will be roast dishes available should you want them. The bar is open at the moment, but closes at three o'clock. Should you want any alcoholic beverages, even when the bar is shut, then you only need to call reception on your room telephone there and they will be brought up to you.

'I could do with a drink after our long drive,' Bill told her, 'so I might just nip down to the bar while my wife unpacks.'

The receptionist continued to explain the hotel facilities. 'The bathroom is just along the hall and as you will be the only guests staying on this floor, you will effectively have sole use of it, which I'm sure will come in handy with you having the two boys. Anything else you need, or if you have any questions, just call reception.' With that, she and the porter left and Bill followed them out of the room. He wanted to check out the hotel bar.

The first three days at Paignton passed very quickly. The hotel staff couldn't do enough for them and they were treated like royalty. It was a different world to what they were used to, but they thoroughly enjoyed being pampered. The boys had a great time going up and down in one of the lifts on their own and even when this began to inconvenience some of the other hotel guests, the staff still showed considerable tolerance. The hotel food was the best they had ever eaten and everything about their stay was just about perfect. Even the weather obliged and they were able to spend hours on the beach, or in one of the hotel's swimming pools. It all seemed to be too good to be true and yet nothing came along to spoil the wonderful time they were having. That was until the Thursday.

They had spent the morning at the beach and had just returned to the hotel for lunch. There seemed to be a bit of a panic going on and Bill wondered what could have happened. They were just about to go up to their suite to change out of their beachwear when the receptionist rushed over to speak to them.

'I'm afraid I've got some bad news for you,' she said. 'The road workmen at the back of the hotel ruptured the water main and in trying to repair it, only made matters worse. Apparently, they can't now stop the water pouring out from the pipe.'

'So, the hotel's water supply has had to be turned off, is that what you are saying?' Bill asked. 'That's not too serious a problem and we've certainly had to put up with a lot worse than that.'

'But sir,' she said. 'It's not the hotel's water supply that is the problem. It's where the water went that is causing us such concern.'

'So where did it go?' he asked

'It flooded the road behind the hotel and then poured down the ramp leading to our underground car park. The water level in there is up to eighteen inches already and from what I understand, it is still rising.'

'But my car is in there!' Bill almost screamed. 'Are you telling me that my Anglia is now under water?'

'I'm afraid so, sir.'

He ran to the lift and pressed the button for the basement level. It was only a short descent and as the doors opened when it stopped, water instantly poured in. He found himself up to his knees in a matter of seconds and started wading through the water to enter the flooded car park, which had all the appearance of a lake. His beloved Anglia was right there in the middle of it, looking like a stranded whale. All the wheels and tyres were almost completely submerged already and as he glanced over towards the ramp, he could see a veritable torrent of water still cascading down it. He was absolutely horrified. He had expected this car park to be a safe place for him to leave his new car, but instead of that, it had turned into a subterranean water trap, with his Anglia as its victim. There were a few other cars in there as well, but they weren't his problem. His sole concern was his own car, which was now gradually beginning to disappear as the water level continued to rise.

Bill had never felt so helpless before in his life. The floor on which he was standing was a good five feet below the level of the road surface outside and unless the flow of water ceased, this entire area could flood to that depth. There had to be some drains in this garage, but they were never designed to cope with anything like this. He knew that his Anglia was only fifty-six and three quarters inches high, so there was the distinct possibility that it could end up completely submerged. He just didn't know what to do.

A fireman wearing waders sploshed his way down the ramp and walked over to where Bill was standing. 'Bit of a mess, isn't it?' he said. 'Is that your car?' pointing to the Anglia. Bill was so lost for words that he could only nod his head. 'Well the water level shouldn't rise much more now. My men are currently isolating this whole section of the mains supply pipe and that will stop any more coming in here. Then we'll get some pumps in and drain this lot away in no time at all.'

Bill waded over to the Anglia and peered in through the windows. He couldn't see any water inside, but decided to check to make sure. He fished the keys out of his pocket and unlocked the driver's door. The fireman yelled across, 'Don't open that door, sir!' just a fraction of a second too late. Water poured in, even though the door was only slightly open, and the interior of the car was now just as wet as the outside. It was a really stupid thing to do, but Bill hadn't been thinking clearly at that moment.

A few hours later, the car park had been pumped dry and Bill, who had spent quite some time in the hotel bar by then, returned to have another look at his beloved Anglia. He had changed out of his beach attire and was now wearing a shirt, trousers, socks and shoes. Several pints of beer and a few large whiskies had left him a little intoxicated and on another thoughtless impulse, he opened the car door. The water inside promptly flooded out over his feet, soaking his shoes and socks. In his anger, he kicked the door shut, which made the second time in the same day that the Anglia had been attacked. He was now in a foul mood. His special holiday for the family had turned into a complete disaster and goodness knows what he was supposed to do now. The inside of what had been his pride and joy was now full of water and the entire lower half of the car had been completely submerged for several hours. On top of all that, he was still over a hundred miles from home. He returned to their suite to sleep off the effects of the alcohol.

Their evening meal was eaten in virtually complete silence. Deidre had told the boys not to even try to speak to their father and they weren't about to ignore her warning. Bill had a bad headache, although that was his own fault, and the only pair of decent shoes he had brought along for their holiday were now soaking wet. Until they dried out, he would have to make do with wearing flip-flops all the time. The manager of the hotel had profusely apologised to him about the damage caused to his car as a result of the garage being flooded, although it obviously wasn't his fault. The person to blame was whichever of the road workers had stupidly decided to stick his pick axe through the water main and Bill would have dearly loved to have got his hands around that man's throat.

'Our insurance will cover the cost of putting your car right,' the manager said, 'so you have no need to worry about that.'

'That may be,' Bill told him, 'but it was a brand new car and to have something like this happen to it.'

The following morning, a man from one of the local garages turned up to have a look at the Anglia. He seemed amused when he saw water sloshing around in the rear footwells and laughingly asked Bill which idiot had opened one of the doors. 'I did,' he was told. 'I know it was a stupid thing to do but I wasn't thinking straight at the time.

'Well, if you hadn't,' the man said, now adopting a

more serious tone, 'the rest of the car would have dried out pretty quickly on its own, but now that the carpets are all soaked, they will need to be taken out and dry cleaned and that's going to take a few days.'

'So, what do you suggest I do?'

'Well, as you are only here for another couple of days, I'd be tempted to drive the car home and get it sorted out back there. It wasn't under water for that long, so it will still be driveable. We could clean it all up for you, but that would mean you having to stay here and that may not be altogether convenient.'

'I don't suppose you come across this sort of thing very often.' Bill suggested to the garage man.

'Happens all the time, mate. People leave their cars at the beach car park without realising that it gets flooded when the tide comes in. We usually get one or two a month and more during the holiday season. In a way though, you were quite lucky,' he added. 'The ones on the beach get flooded by sea water and that's very corrosive. Those cars inevitably start to rust very soon afterwards. In your case it was fresh water, so it could have been a lot worse. You might get some rust starting, so will need to keep an eye out for that, but this is a new car so you should be alright.'

On the Saturday morning, Bill drove the family home. The carpets made a squishy noise every time anybody moved their feet and there was a definite smell of dampness inside the car. There was also the dent in the driver's door which would need to be fixed, but Bill's love affair with his Ford Anglia Super was now over. To him, it was never going to be the same car again and that single incident in Paignton was to completely change the Anglia's future.

## 13

## THE JOURNEY HOME

The journey home was both slow and painful, but at least there wasn't water splashing about on the floor of the car. The hotel manager had arranged for two of his cleaning ladies to empty it out as best they could and although they couldn't do much about the soaking wet carpets, they did get the majority of the water out. Fortunately, the car door hadn't been open for more than a couple of seconds, so the level in the car hadn't risen high enough to get the seats wet, which was something. The last thing Bill needed was to have to drive home with the boys squirming about on the back seat, complaining about having wet botties.

'It could have been worse,' Deidre said, trying to relieve the obvious tension in the car. 'If the firemen hadn't managed to turn the water off when they did, the level might have risen right up to the roof of the car and think what sort of a state it would have been in then. At least it's only the carpets that got wet and they can be dried out.'

'It's not just the carpets,' he told her. 'The wheels were completely under water and the brake shoes got soaked through. They'll dry out fairly quickly but aren't working properly yet, as I need to press really hard on the pedal to get the car to slow down. All the wheels and drums will need to come off to be looked at and new brake shoes will probably have to be fitted. Don't forget that the engine was half submerged as well and goodness knows what damage that will have done.'

'But everything can all be fixed,' she said, 'and it won't cost you anything because the hotel's insurance will pay for all necessary repairs.'

'Yes, but the Anglia will never be the same as it was before this happened. It was brand new and there wasn't a mark on it. Now it's damaged goods and that makes all the difference.'

'Don't you love this beautiful car anymore, Daddy?' Colin piped up from the back seat.

Both Bill and Deidre shouted, 'Shut up Colin,' at exactly the same moment. Nobody said a word after that and the journey continued in complete silence. Getting a puncture just outside Yeovil didn't help matters at all. Bill saw the broken glass on the road ahead of him and tried to brake to avoid running over it, but the brakes didn't respond quickly enough and he drove straight through it. It was the front nearside tyre that was punctured and he felt it immediately in the way the car handled. He slammed his fists against the rim of the steering wheel and swore.

There was a lay-by just ahead, so he pulled into that and ordered everybody out of the car. Deidre took the boys a short distance away, so they wouldn't hear the language their dad might use while he was working on the car.

Having dragged the spare wheel, jack and wheel brace out of the boot, Bill set about changing the wheel. The hub cap came off easily enough, as did the wheel trim, but the wheel nuts refused to move. They had been done up really tight in the Ford plant at Halewood and the wheel brace supplied with the car didn't seem man enough to shift them, or maybe it was just that he wasn't strong enough. He cursed the fact that he hadn't brought his toolkit with him on the trip, as there would have been something in there that he could have used to loosen the reluctant nuts. He swore again, justifying Deidre's decision to take the boys out of earshot.

He only finally managed to shift them by standing on the handle of the wheel brace and using the power he had in his legs. Even so, it still took some time before he freed the last one. The jack was already in position so he turned the ratchet and lifted the car until the front tyre was completely off the ground. He then unscrewed the loosened wheel nuts the rest of the way and changed the wheel. When the Anglia was back on the ground again, he returned the wheel with the punctured tyre to the boot and stowed away the jack and wheel brace. As he had needed to completely empty the boot to get the spare wheel out, he now piled their suitcases back into it and slammed the lid. 'Come on you lot,' he shouted to Deidre and the boys. 'Let's go home before something else goes wrong!'

Bill had obviously ensured that the wheel nuts were properly tightened as soon as he had lowered the car and removed the jack. Only a complete idiot would forget to do something like that, but there was one thing he had forgotten to do. As the Anglia roared off up the road, taking the family away from this scene of so much bad language, the hub cap and wheel trim remained exactly where he had left them sitting on the ground in the lay-by. He hadn't remembered to put them back on, but wouldn't realise this until sometime later.

Further into the journey, another Anglia passed them

going the opposite way and its driver flashed his lights and tooted his horn to greet a fellow owner. Bill just ignored him and stamped his foot down on the throttle. The thought going through his mind was that the sooner this journey was over, the better.

When he heard the clanging sound of a bell and looked in his rear view mirror, Bill wasn't altogether surprised to see a police car on his tail. It was a big black Mark III Ford Zephyr and the blue light on top of its roof was flashing. He glanced down at his speedometer and swore again. He was doing sixty-five miles per hour and was in a fifty limit. He cruised to a halt and waited for the inevitable appearance of a police officer at his side window.

'Do you know why I stopped you?' the policeman asked.

'I've no idea,' Bill told him. 'I was just driving along minding my own business and as far as I'm aware, I wasn't breaking the law in any way.'

'And how fast do you think you were going?'

'About forty-five, fifty, I suppose. I don't think I was going any faster than that.'

'The needle on that big dial in front of you said sixty-five, daddy,' came Colin's voice from the back seat. 'I was watching it over your shoulder.'

The policeman glanced at the boy and then turned back to Bill. 'Perhaps you would like to show me your driving license and insurance certificate, sir?' It had sounded like a polite request, but Bill knew better. He handed over the documents, which the policeman then studied for a moment. Still holding them in his hand, he began walking round the Anglia, checking for anything to indicate that the car wasn't roadworthy. He paused at the front nearside wheel, before returning to the driver's door.

'Did you know that you are missing the hub cap and trim from your front wheel, sir?' he asked.

The expression of surprise on Bill's face answered his question, as the sudden realisation that he had forgotten to put them back on after changing the wheel at the lay-by came to him. He explained what had happened to the police officer and for good measure, added about the car getting submerged in the hotel underground car park at Paignton.

'Not having much luck recently, are you sir?' the officer said, 'and now I've caught you doing sixty-five in a fifty mile an hour limit! Would you mind stepping out of the car please?'

Bill climbed out and stood there in his flip-flops. The hint of a smile appeared on the policeman's face when he saw what he was wearing on his feet. He leaned into the car and touched the carpet with his hand. It came away wet, confirming what Bill had told him. 'How long have you had this car, sir?' he asked.

'I got it two weeks ago. It was brand new when I bought it.'

The policeman didn't say anything for a moment or two, but then gave Bill back his license and insurance certificate. 'The last thing you need to add to the problems you've obviously been having recently is a speeding ticket, so I'm going to let you off with a warning on this occasion. You're free to get on your way, but please watch your speed in future, sir!'

Bill thanked the officer profusely and then climbed back into the car. He started the engine and after engaging first gear, drove off. The policeman waved goodbye to them and then returned to his Zephyr.

Bill knew that he'd been lucky and although he wasn't at all pleased with Colin for blurting out his actual speed, he knew the boy was only doing what he'd been taught to do, which was to always tell the truth, so he couldn't really punish him for that. The hub cap and trim he'd left at the lay-by near Yeovil would just have to stay there now, as he had no intention of driving the thirty odd miles back to get them. For the rest of the journey home, he carefully observed all the speed limits.

When they finally arrived home, Bill got out of the Anglia and went and opened the front door to the house. It was just past one thirty, so there would be time for him to get a quick pint at his local if he hurried. He went back to get their suitcases from the boot. Deidre had also got out of the car by now and was helping the two boys out. They ran straight into the house, as they were keen to get upstairs to play with their train set. He dragged the cases indoors and dumped them on the floor of the lounge. Deidre could start unpacking them and sorting out the things that would need to be taken to the launderette while he went off to the pub. He hadn't enjoyed the trip home and was annoyed at himself for having forgotten to put the hub cap and wheel trim back on, but at least the police officer hadn't given him the speeding ticket he'd so richly deserved, so he was at least grateful for that.

As he walked past the Anglia on his way to the pub, he stopped for a moment to look at it. Its bodywork and chrome still shone every bit as brightly as it had done before and there was nothing to show that it had spent several hours submerged in water. He knew it was a different story on the inside, but that was his own stupid fault. He had noticed that by the time they'd arrived home the brakes seemed to be working properly again, so the shoes must have dried out with the heat generated by the friction caused when he kept using them. They would still need to be checked out though, but that would be a job for the garage.

Had it not been for the incident in Paignton, he would not now be visiting the pub, but be busy cleaning and polishing the Anglia in preparation for putting it away in the garage, but he had lost all interest in doing that. First things first and right at this moment, the thing he wanted most was a pint of beer. He needed it after that tedious and frustrating journey home. He might feel better once he had got one or two of them inside him and they might even help him forget the events of the last few days. He would possibly think about cleaning the Anglia when he got back from the pub but then again, maybe he wouldn't bother.

All the euphoria he had previously felt about being the proud owner of a Ford Anglia Super was now gone. It was just a car after all and he would never lavish the care and attention on it that he would have done, had things been different. His dream car would have been cherished and mollycoddled and maintained in perfect condition, which was what it really deserved, but now he didn't really care. Whilst driving back, he had even considered selling it back to the Ford Dealership in Salisbury, but knew that he would lose an awful lot of money if he did that. He really had no choice but to keep the thing but it would be just a means of transport and not his dream machine. The bubble had burst and from now on, the Ford Anglia Super would have to take its chances like every other car on the road. It might have had a golden future but unfortunately, that wasn't the case now. The seeds of the Anglia's gradual decline into becoming a rusty old heap rotting away in a garage had been sown and the car's future was now written.

# 14

# THE DRIVING LESSON

The following morning, Bill took all the removable carpets out of the car and put them on the front lawn. The sun would help dry them out a bit, but that still left the rest of the carpeting inside the Anglia and he would need to remove the front seats if he wanted to get that out as well. The section over the gearbox cover was now only a bit damp at the bottom, so he wasn't overly concerned about that part, but the carpeting under the seats had been totally immersed in water and that would need to be dealt with.

The hotel manager had said that their insurance would pay for any repairs to the Anglia, so Bill decided that it wasn't really worth him trying to sort out all the fitted carpeting himself. He would simply take the car back to the dealers where he'd bought it and instruct them to do whatever was necessary to repair the damage. If they decided that any of the carpeting needed replacing, then that would be the insurance company's problem, not his. This would mean taking some more time off work, but hopefully his bosses would understand the problem he was faced with.

At nine o'clock on the Monday morning, he drove into the workshop yard behind the dealers and asked to speak to the manager of the service department.

'Good morning,' the man said. 'How can I help you?'

'I need you guys to have a look at my car,' Bill told him, indicating the Anglia in its parking spot. 'It became trapped in a flooded underground garage and got rather wet inside.'

The manager recognised the car immediately, as it had been in his workshop a fortnight or so earlier to have its number plates fitted. 'How very unfortunate, sir' he said, 'but I'm sure we'll be able to sort that out for you. 'How high did the water level rise?

Bill explained what had happened, but neglected to mention that he was the idiot who had opened the door to let the water into the car. 'The hotel's insurance is going to pay for any repairs, so I've written down the name of the manager there and the hotel's address and telephone number for you.' He handed over the slip of paper on which he'd written these details. 'I will leave the car with you if that's okay and you will just have to let me know when it has all been sorted out.'

The workshop manager glanced at the piece of paper in his hand and saw that Bill had also written down the name and telephone number of the factory where he worked as a contact point during the day. 'What we could do when the work has been completed, sir,' he told Bill, 'is to deliver the car to your place of work, if that would be of any assistance to you.'

'That would be most helpful, thank you.'

His two week's old ex-dream car was accordingly left with the workshop staff and Bill walked back to the factory to clock on. He would have to take the bus home after work, but as he hadn't got rid of the old Standard Eight yet, he would be able to use that to get to and from work for however long it took for the Anglia's repairs to be carried out, which the manager had said shouldn't be more than three to four days. It was just as well that he hadn't got around to cancelling the insurance on the Standard yet and that it still had a month's road tax left.

When the car was returned to him, the mechanic who delivered it told him that all the carpeting within the car had been replaced. 'There was just too much shrinkage after it had all been thoroughly cleaned and dried,' he said, 'so we had to replace the carpets throughout. The inside is as good as new again now and we've also checked the engine compartment and boot for any possible water damage there. The brakes were stripped out and cleaned and all the joints in the suspension and steering have been inspected in case any water got into any of them. All the joints were then fully lubricated, so your Anglia Super has now been returned to showroom condition.'

'You have obviously been very thorough,' Bill said, 'but as I told the wife, it is never going to be quite the same to me as it was before. I can't really explain why I feel like that, but it was my dream car and now it's different in some way.'

'But it is only three weeks old with less than six hundred miles on the clock and is in perfect condition,' the mechanic pointed out. 'To all intents and purposes it is still a brand new car, so I can't see what your problem is.'

'I realise that and as I said, I can't explain it, but all the magic has somehow gone out of this car for me.'

'Well, I can't help you there I'm afraid,' the mechanic told him. 'I just wish I could afford to buy a car like yours for myself.'

But Bill's mind was now set and the Anglia Super

would no longer be pampered as the car of his dreams.

As time went on, he did occasionally wash his Anglia, but only to get off the surface muck and it was never put away in the garage at night. He had even bought himself a tin of wax polish when they were in Paignton, so that he could take proper care of the car's shiny bodywork, but this was never even opened. The one thing he did do however was to check the oil and tyre pressures occasionally but apart from that, he paid precious little attention to the car's maintenance. The Standard Eight, which he finally sold for eight pounds, used to get more time spent on it than the Anglia ever did or would.

Deidre just couldn't understand why he seemed so disenchanted with the car and nagged him constantly, but all to no avail. He just didn't care anymore and nothing she said seemed to get through. He did finally get around to fitting some seat covers to protect the surfaces of the front seats, but only because she had bought him a set for his birthday and kept going on at him until he did fit them.

It was all a terrible shame and the Anglia deserved better, but it was at the beginning of the downward spiral that would eventually lead to an ignominious end.

Deidre hadn't forgotten what she had said about learning to drive and broached the subject again.

'I'm still thinking about learning how to drive,' she said one evening, 'so I am going to book myself in for a couple of lessons. Gloria went to the BSM when she learnt and says they're very good, so I might give them a try.'

'I think you should do that,' Bill told her, 'and when you've had a few lessons, I will probably let you have a go at driving the Anglia, to see how you get on with it.'

The fact that he would consider letting her anywhere near his car as a learner driver was further evidence, if any was required, of how little the Anglia now meant to him. He had been so adamant on that first day that he didn't want her to drive it as a learner, but now it didn't seem to bother him.

A few weeks later, Bill drove her to an old abandoned airfield some miles to the west of Salisbury. He wasn't to know that this was the same airfield that Mr. X had taken off from on his doomed flight. They were both sitting in the Anglia with Deidre in the driver's seat. 'Now all I want you to do,' he said, 'is to move off smoothly and follow this track around the airfield. Don't go too fast and try to keep it as smooth as you possibly can.' Deidre engaged first gear and released the clutch.

The car leapt forward with a bound, the Anglia giving a very passable impression of a startled kangaroo. Bill wondered what it was about the word 'smooth' that she didn't seem to understand. Rather than make her panic by shouting at her, he grabbed hold of the dashboard for support and kept his mouth shut.

The car settled down and the ride became more even. Her changing up into second gear wasn't accomplished smoothly or quietly but she found it eventually and they began to accelerate. She seemed to be getting the hang of changing gear by the time she selected third, but forgot that she also needed to steer the car at the same time. The Anglia began to wander about and Bill had to reach across and grab the steering wheel to correct her course on a number of occasions.

By now, they were really beginning to pick up speed

and he began to get nervous, particularly when she took her eyes off the road completely. She was staring at the gear lever and seemed to be trying to work out where she needed to push it to find fourth gear.

'Watch the road!' he shouted, but it was too late. They veered off the track and were now bouncing along the grass verge.

'Don't you shout at me!' she yelled, before slamming on the brakes. Bill was thrown forwards and only just managed to avoid hitting the windscreen. As she hadn't remembered to depress the clutch pedal when she stood on the brakes, the Anglia had juddered to a standstill and was now stalled. Bill fell back into his seat and turned to face her. Deidre was sitting there with her arms crossed and a very upset expression on her face. He could tell she was seething with anger and waited for the inevitable explosion that he knew was about to come. The fact that they were off the road completely, with the car stalled in third gear, was all going to be his fault, there was no doubt about it.

'I'm sorry I shouted at you,' he said, in the kindest tone he could, 'but you must remember to watch where you're going at all times.'

No response from Deidre.

'But there's no harm done love,' he told her. 'Let's just get back on the road itself and then you can have another go.'

The lesson continued and at Bill's suggestion, Deidre stayed in second gear, to allow her to concentrate on learning to steer properly. After a while, she seemed to have got some of her confidence back and he suggested that she should change into third. This she attempted to do by feel, rather than by looking at the gear lever, as her eyes were now firmly fixed on the road ahead. Unfortunately, this took so long that by the time she had finally found third, the car's speed had decreased to the point where it was going too slow to be in that gear. It juddered along for a bit and then stalled again.

'Why did it do that?' she asked him. 'I thought I was doing everything right.'

'It only happened because you let the car's speed drop too much,' he told her. 'You must maintain momentum and also keep the revs up when you're changing up into a higher gear. You will only be able to do that if your gear changes are dealt with smoothly and quickly.'

'There is just so much to learn,' she said. 'I don't think I'm ever going to get the hang of it.'

'You are doing really well,' he said encouragingly. 'Bear in mind that this is the first time you've ever driven the Anglia.'

They continued for another half hour or so by which time Bill felt that he couldn't take any more. He called it a day and proposed that they should return home. Deidre stopped the car and got out, allowing him to take over the driving. He had been dreading that she might suggest driving them home herself, as he didn't think his nerves could possibly survive the journey, if she had to contend with other road users as well as trying to control the car.

The lesson had ended with no injuries to either of them and no damage done to the car. But it did give Bill new respect for driving instructors and what they had to put up with on a daily basis. They regularly took their lives in their hands with learner drivers on the open road and he would never have the courage for that job.

After a few months, quite a few more lessons and

several sessions at the airfield, Deidre actually managed to pass her driving test at the first attempt. This meant that there were now two drivers in the family and she could share the driving whenever they went anywhere. It had all been worthwhile in the end, but it would be a very long time before Bill forgot his nerve-wracking experiences with her and that airfield.

When Bill bought the Anglia, he was looking forward to seven years of motoring before he would need to worry about taking the car for its first MOT test, but that was before they changed the rules. In April 1967, the Secretary of State for Transport, formerly known as the Minister of Transport, decided that seven years was too long a period and reduced it to three years.

Many drivers who owned cars that were between three and seven years old complained bitterly when Barbara Castle announced this change, but there was nothing they could do about it. Bill was every bit as put out as the rest of them, as it meant that his Anglia would have to have an MOT test that year and every subsequent year. It wasn't that he was worried about it passing, but he'd thought he had left all that behind him and didn't expect to need to take the Anglia to be tested until 1971. He duly submitted it for its first MOT test in the August and it sailed through without any problems.

This was the second time he'd been caught out in this way, as exactly the same thing had happened to him when he owned the old Standard. He just seemed to be fated when it came to MOT tests and it would be a future MOT test would hammer the final nail in the coffin of his Ford Anglia Super.

# 15

# A LITTLE DRIVE IN THE CAR

The swinging sixties ended and it was the beginning of the seventies. Christopher had just become a teenager and Colin was now fourteen. An Act passed in 1969 reduced the age of majority from twenty-one to eighteen years of age, so he would now become eligible to vote in just four years time. Gone were the days when Bill could get away with giving the boys half a crown each a week as pocket money and that coin itself ceased to be legal tender on 1st January 1970.

The Anglia Super was now coming up to six years old. Its painted bodywork had lost some of its sheen, but it still looked in good condition, considering how little care and attention Bill was giving it. It had needed to have four new tyres fitted a year or so previously but other than that, it hadn't involved him in any major expenditure and had proved to be reliable. The Anglia model had by then been out of production for nearly three years and its replacement, the Ford Escort, was selling well in 1970. Other Fords available at the time were the Capri and the Cortina Mark II, which would be replaced later in the year by the Mark III Cortina.

Dixon of Dock Green was still on the telly, so Deidre was happy, and Colin and Christopher were getting into a recently released new comedy series called 'Monty Python's Flying Circus' on the Beeb. Bill spent most of his free time either working in the garden or at his allotment, although working there was so exhausting that he always had to call into the pub on his way home, just to build up his strength again.

'I really worked hard at the allotment this morning and got very tired,' he told Deidre, when he came home shortly after the pubs shut one Sunday afternoon.

'Yes, I can smell it on your breath,' Deidre told him. 'How many did you have, two or three?'

'I think it was three, I'm not quite sure now.'

'Well, you'll be no use to anyone for the rest of the day. Why don't you go upstairs and have a nap.'

Bill was swaying slightly as he left the room, leaving Deidre alone in the lounge. She had already prepared the vegetables for their evening meal, so all that was now required was to cook them and to boil the gammon in a pot on the stove for an hour or so for their food to be ready. That gave her a few hours of peace and quiet and she wondered how best to enjoy it. She decided to go out for a drive.

Deidre had driven the Anglia many times by then, but this had always been with Bill sitting beside her. She had never actually gone out on her own in it and this was an experience she'd been promising herself for quite some time. She didn't have any concerns about Bill not being in the car with her, as she had no doubts whatsoever about her driving skills, and it would make a pleasant change knowing that he wasn't there watching her every move. She always felt that he was just waiting for her to make a mistake of some sort so that he could comment on it. He had rarely actually said anything about her driving, but she had seen him pressing his foot down on an imaginary brake pedal on his side of the car, whenever he had thought she wasn't braking early enough. He had done this on a number of occasions and it always annoyed her whenever he did so.

She couldn't decide quite where to go but then had an inspiration. She would go to that old airfield where she had driven the Anglia for the very first time. It would be like a bit of nostalgia for her to go there again, but now she could drive around it full of confidence. She grabbed her handbag and the car keys off the sideboard.

The disused airfield belonged to a farmer and he used it as a place to store fertiliser, in the form of great big heaps of dung. He also kept stacked bales of hay there, as well as some odd bits of farming equipment. Deidre had never seen anyone else at the airfield in all the times she had visited the place with Bill and was quite surprised to see another car there when she arrived. It was a dark blue Ford Cortina and was parked next to one of the dilapidated old cinderblock buildings left over from the war. There was no sign of its owner, so she assumed that whoever drove it there must be inside the building. Whatever it was doing there was none of her business so she chose to ignore it.

As she was driving around, making sure that she avoided hitting any of the stacks of hay and particularly the dung heaps, she was really beginning to enjoy herself. Bill would have had kittens if he'd been in the car with her, as she was often driving much faster than she would have dared go when he was trying to teach her how to drive.

She was motoring along a straight section of road when she happened to look up at the rear view mirror. All her confidence vanished in an instant, to be replaced by sheer panic. There was a light aircraft right behind her and its shape completely filled her mirror. It wasn't more than a few feet off the ground and was obviously coming in to land. Although the aircraft's fuselage was off to one side of her, she could tell that its port wing was going to pass directly over the Anglia. She hit the brakes and performed an emergency stop that would have satisfied any driving test examiner.

The plane flew directly over her, literally just feet above the roof, and landed a short distance further on. Deidre sat there shaking like a leaf for more than a minute. She had never been so scared in her life. She knew that its pilot must have seen the car, but he had clearly decided to completely ignore it and continue with his landing approach. She intended to have a few words with that pilot.

Two men came out of the derelict building and began to approach the plane. They stopped in their tracks when they saw the stationary Anglia a short distance away and seemed undecided as to what to do. By now, the pilot was beginning to climb out of the plane and he yelled something at them.

One of them ran towards the Anglia and the next thing Deidre knew, he was standing right there by the driver's door. She couldn't see his features, as he had pulled his scarf up to hide the lower part of his face, but what she could clearly see was that he was holding a very large gun in his hand.

'Get out of the car, lady' he shouted, waving the pistol at her as if to emphasise the point.

Deidre didn't know what to do. She was alone in the car, miles from the nearest house and any chance of help. She thought about locking the driver's door from the inside, but then remembered that you couldn't do that in the Anglia. Only the passenger door could be locked from inside. She could try hanging on to the handle in the hope that this would prevent the man from opening the door, but then he could just as easily shoot her through the window. Her best chance had to be to comply, so she reached for the handle and opened the car door. The man with the gun stepped back as she slowly climbed out of the Anglia.

As she stood there terrified, Deidre glanced across at the plane and saw that its pilot and the other man were now busy unloading packages from the aircraft and putting them into the boot of the Cortina. She had no idea what was in them, but everything suggested that what was happening here had to be highly illegal. Her little jaunt in the Anglia had dropped her right in the middle of some criminal activity and she was now in a very dangerous situation.

'What are you doing here?' the man with the gun demanded.

'I was just out for a drive,' she told him, her voice shaking with the fear she felt. 'I don't know what is going on here and I don't want to know. Just let me go and I promise I won't say anything.'

'Not a chance!' he retorted. His tone sending shivers up and down Deidre's spine.

He reached into the car and removed the keys from the ignition. Motioning at her with his gun, he said, 'You just sit there quietly until we decide what to do with you. Don't even think about making a run for it, because I will shoot you if you try anything like that!'

Deidre did what she was told and the man went back to join the others. She could see that they were having a heated discussion, most probably about what they were going to do about her. Eventually, they seemed to come to a conclusion. The pilot climbed back into his aircraft and started up the engine. The other two then took hold of its tail plane and moved the aircraft round until it was facing the direction from which it had come. The engine was revved up and it began to roll forwards, quickly picking up speed. As it passed the Anglia, Deidre saw the pilot look in her direction. He made a gesture with his hand, as if he was cutting his own throat, and she didn't need to be told what that meant. The plane took off and climbed up into the sky.

The other two men were now standing by the Cortina watching its departure. They then began talking with one another. Deidre now knew that they intended to kill her and they were probably trying to decide which of them was actually going to do the deed.

It seemed totally unbelievable that was meant to be a fun drive round the airfield had suddenly become a deadly situation, but this is what it now was and what made this even worse, was that she knew there wasn't a thing she could do about it. She reached across to her handbag on the passenger seat to get a hankie. One of the men was now climbing back into the Cortina and the other one turned to face the Anglia.

Deidre couldn't take her eyes off her executioner as he slowly walked towards her, checking his gun as he did so. She blindly fumbled in the handbag desperately trying to find her hankie, but suddenly found something else instead. It was her own set of keys for the Anglia. She had picked up Bill's from the sideboard when she left the house, not thinking about the ones she kept in her handbag. Perhaps there was still a chance of escape.

She quickly pulled the keys out and after inserting the right one into the ignition, fired the engine and selected reverse gear. It wasn't the smoothest transition from stationary to rapid movement, but it took the gunman by surprise. As the Anglia hurtled backwards, he raised his pistol and fired. Either he wasn't much of a marksman or he hadn't aimed properly in his haste to get off a shot, but the bullet missed the car completely. He raced back to the Cortina and jumped into the passenger seat.

Deidre hadn't seen any of this as she was too busy concentrating on trying to steer the car as it raced backwards along the road. She had watched car chases on the telly, where the driver did a handbrake turn to reverse a car's direction, but she didn't have a clue how to do that. What she did know however was that she would need to turn the car around if she was to have any chance at all of escaping. A three-point turn was out of the question, as there wouldn't be enough time for such a slow manoeuvre, so she would need to think of some other way to get the car going forwards instead of backwards.

An opportunity presented itself when she came to one of the large concreted areas where the farmer stacked his hay bales. It was roughly square in shape and had three roads leading to it. She slammed on the brakes and stopped just before piling into one of the haystacks. As she turned to face the front again, she was horrified the see the Cortina heading straight at her. With first gear selected, Deidre gunned the engine and took off, taking the road to her right.

The crooks in their speeding car had been intent on ramming her, but she had somehow managed to get out of the way in time. They were going much too fast to stop before they hit the haystack and when they slammed into it, bales of hay cascaded down on top of the Cortina. This didn't slow them down much, as the driver simply reversed out from underneath the fallen bales and then took off after the Anglia again.

Driving much faster than she knew was wise, Deidre literally threw the car round corners and kept her foot pressed down hard on the throttle. The Cortina couldn't catch her, although it was never far behind. It seemed to be having more trouble negotiating the tight corners at speed than the Anglia was having and any advantage it gained on the straights, it lost again when they came to the next corner. Deirdre was somehow managing to outdrive the crooks, but it could only be a matter of time before one or other of the cars crashed.

She could see a huge pile of rotting dung directly ahead of her and it looked as if this particular road came to a dead-end at that point. Any thoughts of slowing down were immediately dispelled when she glanced in her rear view mirror. The Cortina was right on her tail. All she could do was to trust the Anglia's road holding and at the very last moment, threw the steering wheel hard over to the left. Miraculously, there was a road there. It was so overgrown as to be virtually invisible, but the Anglia managed to take the corner, albeit with some difficulty. Her suddenly swerving off was the last thing the crooks had expected, as they thought they'd finally got her cornered on this dead-end road. They piled straight into the huge dung heap without even noticeably slowing down. There was no chance of the Cortina reversing out of the mess it was in now.

Deidre continued at a slower pace, heading for the road that provided access to the airfield. When she got there, she found several police cars blocking it. They had received a tipoff about a drug shipment being landed here this afternoon and having seen the plane taking off, were now just waiting for the crooks to try to leave the airfield, so that they could catch them red-handed with the drugs.

After Deidre had explained what she'd seen and what had happened afterwards, two police cars drove onto the airfield to apprehend the men in the Cortina. She had told them exactly where they could be found.

'We will require a statement from you,' the inspector said, 'but you are obviously quite shaken up at the moment, so we will leave that for the moment. Will you be able to drive home on your own, or would you like one of my men to accompany you?'

'I will be okay to drive on my own,' Deidre told him. 'Perhaps you could send an officer round to my house later on today to collect my statement, as I really need to be getting home now to deal with the dinner.'

When she arrived home, she found Bill and the boys looking concerned. 'Where on earth have you been?' he asked. 'You didn't leave a note or anything and we had no idea where you'd gone or what might have happened to you.'

'Oh, I'm perfectly fine,' Deidre said. 'I just went out for a little drive in the car.'

# 16

# AN END TO THE DREAM

As the years wore on, the combination of bad winters and Bill not taking proper care of the Anglia began to take their toll. Councils spread salt on the roads in winter to help dissolve any snow and ice on them, but this leaves a slushy mess that gets thrown up by the wheels of vehicles passing through it and gets trapped underneath them. Wheel arches in particular are a good example of where this can happen, but there are many other nooks and crannies on the underside of cars. Under normal circumstances this salty slush will melt away and drip off, but if the temperature remains below zero for any extended period, then this will take quite some time. Putting a car away in a warm garage will hasten the process, although it will leave puddles on the floor, but for a car that is left outside, it can take a very long time indeed. Bill's Anglia Super never saw the inside of his garage again after its trip to Paignton.

The corrosive effect of salty slush on metal cars will cause rust to develop and the worst of it is that this is happening out of sight beneath the car. Getting his car treated with underseal would probably have helped, but Bill didn't bother doing that of course, and then there was also the question of how much corrosion resistance Ford actually built into the car when it was originally assembled.

It doesn't just have to be salty slush in winter for rust to take hold, as any form of dampness beneath a car will have the same effect. Mud is a wonderful material for holding water and can get thrown up and trapped in exactly the same way as slush. A few years exposure to the English weather, with all its rain, snow and slush, combined with muddy roads, will invariably lead to rust forming, unless the car's owner takes preventative measures. Undersealing a car can be beneficial, but the underside also needs to be cleaned off on a regular basis. Failure to do this will inevitably mean that the rust bug will get its teeth into a car's bodywork and once there, it will begin to slowly nibble its way through the metal and weaken the car's structure.

Bill never even saw the underneath of his Ford Anglia Super, let alone have it cleaned off in all the time he owned the car. As such, it goes without saying that little bubbles began to appear in its blue paintwork after a number of years. By then, the dreaded rust bug had been busy nibbling away happily for quite some time and although the car's exterior still appeared to be in very good condition, the Anglia was beginning to rust away from the inside out.

The first few little bubbles in the Anglia's paintwork appeared at the rear of the front wings, closely followed by a few more at the top of the wings, just behind the headlights. Bill didn't pay too much attention to these. He knew what they signified, but the philosophy at the time was that all cars rust and there's not a lot you can do about it. His concern was that the car now tended to wander a bit while being driven and there was excess play in the steering. This probably meant a ball joint problem of some sort and if one or more of them was worn out; it would need to be replaced with a new one.

He had now had his Anglia Super for nearly ten years and since 1967, he had needed to take it for an MOT test every year. That was seven years ago and although it had passed every time so far, there were always that nagging doubt whenever the date for its next MOT test loomed on the horizon.

But for his disinterest in the car, he would probably have sorted out the steering problem himself. He'd had to change one of the track rod ends on the old Standard he used to own, so he knew what was involved when it came to replacing ball joints. True, that was a long time ago, but the steering linkage on the Ford Anglia was much the same as it had been on a Standard Eight. Testing a car's steering had been part of MOT test checks since they were first introduced, so Bill knew that the Anglia would fail its test this year, unless the work was carried out. He decided to ask the garage to inspect and replace the track rods ends if necessary, before they actually carried out the car's MOT test.

Three years later, in 1977, the list of items checked was expanded to include the condition of the body structure and chassis. This significant change meant the end of the road for many older vehicles, which may not have looked all that bad on the outside, but were structurally unsound beneath the surface. Unfortunately, Bill's Anglia Super fell into this category.

'Sorry mate,' the MOT inspector told him. 'There's too much rust at the front end and that makes it an MOT failure under the new rules.'

'I know the front wings are a bit rusty,' Bill told him, 'but that's not structural, is it? I wouldn't have expected the car to fail its MOT because of that.'

'I'm not talking about the outer wings,' the man explained. 'It's your inner wings that are the problem, particularly around the top of the offside front strut. If that area fails, then the entire suspension unit could come up through the bonnet. The nearside one isn't quite so bad, but it won't be long before it is.'

'So, what options does that leave me with?' Bill was now starting to feel a bit concerned.

'Well, you could replace both inner wings, but that would mean a lot of work and with labour costs being what they are these days, doing a job like that would cost you more than the car is worth. It wouldn't be economical for a car this age, as the thing's not worth much anyway. Even if it didn't have all that rust, I think you'd be lucky if you got a hundred quid for it.'

'What else could I do?'

'Your only other option is to scrap it!' the man told him. 'Since these new MOT rules and regulations came in, we've been scrapping a lot of older cars. Yours will be the fifth this month.'

'But its general condition is nothing like bad enough for it to be scrapped, is it?' Bill asked. 'There's hardly a mark on the bodywork, other than the rust on the front wings, and the inside is almost as good as new. There must be some other way to get round the problem.'

The mechanic walked back to the Anglia and started poking at the affected areas with his screwdriver. After a minute or two of this, he looked up and said, 'I suppose we might be able to plate over the top of these struts, after cutting out the worst of the rust. That might do it and it would be considerably cheaper for you.'

'Can you give me any indication of what that's likely to cost?'

'Not off the top of my head,' he replied, 'but give me a couple of days to check out what I can get the bits for and I will let you know.' Bill ended up having to walk home from the garage and to use the bus to get to work for the next week, but the repair work to the Anglia was carried out and it was given an MOT certificate for the next twelve months.

The family's financial situation was now considerably improved on what it had been back in 1964. Colin was now twenty-two years of age and had been working for some years. His younger brother Christopher had also got himself a job and while they both still lived at home, they now paid their mother rent for the privilege of doing so. Bill had become a supervisor at the factory and Deidre had also got a little job for herself, working as a check-out girl at the Co-op. There was now enough money coming in that Bill and Deidre regularly went abroad for their holidays. They still had a couple of years to go on their mortgage, but the amount they were paying wasn't all that much and the house was now worth four times more than what they had paid for it. Deidre also no longer had to take the washing to the launderette, as she now had her own washing machine, as well as a fridge and freezer. Life was comfortable for the family which was probably just as well, as Bill could see himself needing to buy another car in the very near future.

It was time for the Anglia to go, as it was starting to become an expensive liability. With its new MOT certificate, it would be okay for another year, but what would it cost him to have it fixed next year if it failed the MOT test again? It would have to go, but he had no intention of buying a brand new car to replace it. He had made that mistake once and wouldn't do it again. He could still remember seeing his Ford Anglia Super for the very first time, but that was a long time ago. He would never again fall in love with any car and looking back, he was amazed that he had been so smitten with the Anglia in the first place. What he planned to do was to find a good home for it, someone on the lookout for a cheap car, and then there would be a parting of the ways.

A month or so later, Bill got to hear that his niece wanted to buy a car, but didn't want to spend too much money doing so. He decided to give her a call, as they now had their own telephone in the house.

'Rachel, it's your Uncle Bill. Your dad tells me that you've been looking for a car to buy and I'm thinking of getting rid of my old Ford Anglia. I just wondered whether you might be interested in it.'

Rachel was familiar with Uncle Bill's car, as she had seen it many times and had even ridden in it on a few occasions.

'Really?' she said. 'But you've had that car forever. Wasn't that the one you bought when you received that reward money from the bank? I was quite young at the time, but I remember my dad telling me about it.'

'Yes, it's the same one. I bought it in 1964, when you were only about thirteen or fourteen years old. Your aunt and I have decided that it's time we got something younger so if you're interested in it, I will let you have it at a very reasonable price.'

'Well basically,' Rachel told him. 'I just need a cheap second-hand banger. Alan has his car which he uses for going to work, but there are times when I need one for myself, which is why we're looking for a car for me.'

Thirteen years previously, the thought of his treasured Ford Anglia Super ever be considered as a cheap second-hand banger would have absolutely appalled Bill, but the reality of the present situation was that this was what it had now become. He had treated the car shamefully, since that day he became disenchanted with it, but he could only blame himself for that.

Rachel lived in a village in Northamptonshire, about a hundred miles away. She would obviously need to see the Anglia and have a drive in it to see if she liked it, but Bill was quite taken with the idea of the car staying in the family. If Rachel wanted it, then he would sell it to her at a knockdown price and that would be the end of it. His Anglia Super would have a new home and he would have to get something else for himself. They made arrangements for Rachel to come down and see the car the following weekend.

On the Sunday, Rachel arrived with her husband and after a cup of tea and a bit of family chitchat; she went outside with Bill to inspect the Anglia. He had actually bothered to give it a clean, for the first time in ages, so the car really looked quite presentable. The paintwork had obviously faded a bit, but all the chrome trim was still as shiny as ever and there was little about it to show that it was thirteen years old. There were no dents on its bodywork, although the back bumper was pushed in a bit in the middle. Christopher had reversed into a bollard he hadn't seen when he had been learning to drive in the Anglia. The only other dent it had ever had in its long life was when Bill kicked the door shut in Paignton all those years earlier and he'd had to pay for that to be repaired himself, as the hotel's insurance company wasn't prepared to foot the bill.

'It's done sixty-seven thousand miles,' Bill told her, 'but it should be good for a few thousand more before it needs a new engine and everything on the car works exactly how it should. I've just had it MOT'd, but it did need a bit of work done to it, and it's taxed until the middle of December. I only bought four months road tax rather than the full year, because I knew I was going to get rid of it.'

'It looks in amazingly good condition for its age,' said Rachel, running her fingers over the little bubbles in the paintwork on the front wing. I can't really see why you are selling it.'

'Call it a dream that never quite came true,' he said. 'Now, why don't you take the wheel and we can go for a test drive to see how you like driving it.'

Perhaps the Ford Anglia Super was out to impress its potential new owner, because it performed faultlessly. The ride was smooth and comfortable and Rachel had no trouble with any gear changes. The synchromesh on the gearbox was still doing its job and when she pushed down hard on the accelerator, the car proved that it could still produce a good turn of speed if required. The steering felt responsive and the brakes worked efficiently. She was very impressed with the car and couldn't really fault it in any way.

'So, what do you think of it?' Bill asked, after they had returned home.

'I think it's great,' she said. 'How much do you want for it?'

'As you're family, I will let you have the car for forty pounds.'

'I'll take it,' Rachel responded.

And so the deal was struck and what had once been

Bill's dream machine changed hands. The Anglia had only narrowly escaped being scrapped, but now it was destined to have another life, with a new owner. The next chapter in its story was about to be written, but what did the future hold in store for it now?

17

# A CHANGE OF OWNERSHIP

Rachel drove the Anglia home with Alan following her in his car, in case of any problems. This precaution turned out to be totally unnecessary, as the car gave no trouble whatsoever.

It was now October 1977 and Queen's latest release 'We are the Champions' was being played non-stop on Radio One. The actual Queen had celebrated her Silver Jubilee on 7th June that year and the 'King' (Elvis Presley) had finally left the building on 16th August. James Callaghan was the Prime Minister of Britain, having taken over from Harold Wilson eighteen months previously, but it would only be another eighteen months before he too would be packing his bags and leaving Downing Street, heralding in the arrival of Margaret Thatcher and twenty years of successive Conservative governments.

1977 was a really momentous year in terms of things happening, not that any of this concerned the Anglia Super. It was now being cleaned and polished regularly and spent its nights tucked away in a double garage. For the first time in its life, it was being looked after, but this attention had come too late to undo the damage that had already been done by Bill neglecting it. It was fast wearing out and by then, rust had been eating away at it for a good few years. It still looked pretty good on the outside, but its general condition was deteriorating and there was really no way back.

The first problem Rachel had with the Anglia was when the exhaust suddenly became much louder than it should have been. 'It probably needs a new silencer,' her husband told her. 'Take it to the local garage in the morning and get them to have a look at it.'

'It's the exhaust box itself that's actually blowing,' the mechanic at Stowe Hill Garage told her, 'but the entire system is so rusty that it is beginning to fall apart anyway. You really need to change the whole thing.'

A wheel bearing was the next thing to go, followed by the fan belt, which decided to give up the ghost a year or so later. Rachel was happily driving along the road when a tell-tale red light appeared on the instrument panel. Although not mechanically minded, she knew this indicated a problem of some sort, although the car itself still appeared to be running smoothly. She stopped by the side of the road and consulted her owners handbook, which she always kept in the glove box. This advised: 'If the light does not go out before an engine speed equivalent to 15 mph (24 kph) in top gear is reached, a fault in the charging system is indicated and you should consult your nearest Authorised Dealer immediately'.

Rachel didn't know what to make of this. She knew the red light appeared whenever she turned the ignition on and that it went out soon after she started the engine, but the book didn't say what it meant if it suddenly came on while you were driving along. She turned the car around and headed straight for Stow Hill Garage, on the basis that it was better to be safe than sorry.

By the time she got there, the engine was running

lumpily and the needle on the water temperature gauge was right on the 'H' at the top. It usually sat somewhere in the middle between the 'C' and the 'H'. She turned off the engine and pulled the handle on the dashboard to open the bonnet. It always made her smile whenever she did this, as it was labelled 'hood', rather than 'bonnet', which seemed rather odd for a car that had been made in the UK.

The mechanic came out and had a look at the Anglia. 'I can see what's happened,' he said. 'Your fan belt has broken and that's what drives the dynamo and water pump. The reason why the warning light came on is because the battery isn't being charged, but I am a bit concerned that you drove it here, rather than let us come out to you.'

'Why?' she asked. 'I just wanted someone to have a look at it as soon as possible.'

'The reason why you shouldn't have driven it here is because the water pump is what makes water circulate around inside the engine to keep it cool. With that not running, the engine will begin to overheat and that could cause all sorts of problems.'

'Oh!' said Rachel.

The mechanic pulled a large rag out of his pocket and using it to protect his hand, very carefully loosened the radiator filler cap by just a small amount. There was a loud hissing noise and steam began to escape. After a minute or so, he unscrewed the cap the rest of the way. 'You may have boiled the radiator dry, but I can't tell yet,' he told her. 'Hopefully it will be alright, but I will need to let it cool down before I can put any more water in it.'

About twenty minutes or so later, he refilled the

radiator and immediately glanced beneath the car to check for any puddles. There weren't any, so it didn't seem to be leaking, but the acid test would be when the system was re-pressurised. With the new fan belt fitted and properly adjusted, he started the engine and waited for it to warm up. When Rachel asked what he was waiting for, he explained about the thermostat and the fact that water wouldn't begin to circulate around the engine until its temperature was high enough for the thermostat to open.

'What happens then?' she asked.

That is when we will find out for certain whether the radiator leaks or not, once water is flowing through it, but more importantly, I will be able to check to make sure you haven't cracked your block.'

This left Rachel totally confused. She had no idea what her block was, but it had to be something pretty important, if the mechanic was concerned about it.

He saw the puzzled expression on her face and explained. 'The bottom half of this engine is a cast iron block of metal,' he said. 'When an engine gets seriously overheated, usually because the cooling system isn't working properly, then this block can crack and that really is bad news.'

'How bad is bad?'

'About as bad as it can get,' he said. 'It would probably mean you would need to replace the engine.'

'Oh! That bad!'

As it happened, Rachel was extremely fortunate on this occasion. There were no signs of any leaks from either the radiator or the engine. More by luck than judgement, she hadn't driven the car far enough to cause any real damage and the cost of replacing the fan belt was a small price to pay, compared to what the bill might have been. The experience did however teach her a valuable lesson in that she would never again keep driving any car if one of the warning lights came on.

By August 1979, Rachel had owned the Anglia Super for nearly two years and whilst it had been generally reliable, it seemed to be costing her more each year to keep it on the road. She was at Stowe Hill Garage and the car had just had another MOT test, which had meant spending more money on it to pass the test, and it wasn't as if she was driving it all that far either. The MOT certificate in her hand showed the car's mileage to be sixty-nine thousand, eight hundred and two miles, only two thousand or so miles more than when she had bought it.

There was a three year old Mini on the forecourt of the garage, which she thought looked very presentable, so perhaps now was the time to wave goodbye to the old Anglia. The mechanic at the garage had a soft spot for her car. It had been such a constant visitor to the place that he told Rachel he would miss it if she never brought the Anglia in to see him again, but his advice was for her to get something a bit younger, that wouldn't keep costing her money.

She decided to hang on to the Anglia for a while longer. As Christmas approached, so did the expiration date for the car's road tax, which was due for renewal on 1st December. The cost of road tax in 1979 was fifty pounds per annum, or eighteen pounds thirty-five for four months tax. Paying annually meant a saving of five pounds and five pence, so Rachel opted to do this. The car had provided her with trouble-free motoring since its MOT test in August and she hadn't actually needed to spend money on it. Should it need any costly work carried out on it within the next twelve months, then she would get rid of it. She could always return the tax disc and claim a refund for the remainder of the tax period.

So as the year 1979 came to a close, the Anglia Super was running well and was taxed until 30th November 1980, with an MOT certificate up to the 14th August. Providing it didn't break down, it should provide eight months of cost free motoring. If ever there was a time to pass the Anglia on to someone else, then this had to be it.

Rachel's brother Tim had graduated from Cambridge University during the summer of 1979 and was now working in the personnel department of British Leyland, at their Longbridge plant near Birmingham. She knew he was a bit strapped for cash and couldn't afford to buy himself a car, so it occurred to her that he might be just the right person to take the Anglia off her hands. She decided to write him a letter, as there was no way that she could contact him by phone.

Tim wrote back to say that he would certainly be interested in having the Anglia, but pointed out that he didn't have any money.

'I wouldn't expect him to pay me for it anyway,' Rachel told her husband. 'It only cost forty quid to buy in the first place, so I wouldn't dream of charging him anything for it.'

'It has cost you a lot more than forty quid to keep the thing on the road for the last two years,' Alan pointed out, 'plus you've just spent fifty pounds getting the thing taxed.

'True,' she said, 'but Tim is my little brother and he deserves a helping hand.'

And so it was agreed that he should be given the Anglia as a belated Christmas present. In January, Alan drove the car up to Northfield, where Tim was living at the time, and met up with him. On 14th January 1980, Tim became the third owner of the Ford Anglia Super and was given the car, a set of keys, the log book and its current MOT certificate.

'Rachel has spent quite a bit of money on this car over the last two years or so,' Alan told him, 'so she expects you to take good care of it.'

'Oh, I will,' Tim promised. 'It has been in the same family now for more than fifteen years, so it is like a family heirloom being passed on to me to become its guardian. You can assure Rachel that I will look after it really well and always keep this car safe.'

'It has been kept garaged in all the time she's owned it,' Alan told him. 'Have you got a garage here?'

'No, I haven't, but I'm not planning on staying here for much more than a year or so anyway. I'm using this job at British Leyland as a springboard to a much better position somewhere else and as soon as I've gained some experience, I will be moving on and will take the Anglia with me. Wherever I go to, I will definitely want to find somewhere with a garage, so that this family heirloom can have a roof over its head.'

Tim was almost as good as his word in that respect. He did look after the Anglia properly for a while and in August 1980, took it to one of the local garages for its next MOT test, which it got through. In the December of that same year, he visited the local Post Office in Northfield, armed with his insurance certificate and the car's MOT certificate, and taxed it for another year. The cost had increased from fifty to sixty pounds per annum by then, but he had been saving up for some time so that he could afford to pay this.

He used to get a bit of stick from his colleagues at work, as it wasn't really the done thing to turn up at the British Leyland offices every day in a car manufactured by their arch-rivals Ford, but Tim could deal with this and took it all in good humour.

In the summer of 1981, he left British Leyland to take up a position in the personnel department of the Exxon Corporation, at their Fawley refinery on the south coast in Hampshire. This company was originally called the Standard Oil Company but had changed its name to Exxon in 1972. After eighteen months of being parked in the road outside a rented house in Northfield, the Ford Anglia Super was finally moved to somewhere with a garage. Tim had bought a new house in Hythe, Southampton, which was just half an hour's drive away from his office, and his promise that the Anglia would have a roof over its head was about to be fulfilled.

It had proved to be reasonably reliable during the period that Tim had been its guardian and the fortunes of this family heirloom began to look promising once again, but fate can be a cruel mistress and was about deliver the coup de grâce that would seal the Anglia Super's future once and for all.

# 18

# THE END OF THE ROAD

It had taken seventeen years for the Anglia to get a roof over its head again and the irony of the situation was that it was now garaged just twenty-five miles away from its original sheltered location in the Salisbury dealer's showroom. During the intervening years, it had travelled approximately seventy-eight thousand miles and was now on its third owner, all from within the same family.

Tim was the Anglia's owner, but not necessarily its registered keeper. He had been given the log book, which would have had Rachel's name on it, but to register the car in his name, he would have needed to notify the DVLC about the change of ownership. If this was never done, it would mean that Rachel, who thought she'd got rid of the Anglia eighteen months previously, was still officially responsible for the car.

When Tim took the Anglia to the local garage in Hythe for its MOT test in August 1981, he had a nasty surprise coming. What had initially been a few bubbles in the paintwork on the wings was now very obviously a serious rust problem. At the rear of the wings, corrosion had eaten its way into the 'A' pillars on both sides and the outer sills beneath each of the doors were beginning to rust away. The plating repair to the top of the front suspension struts, carried out in 1977, was still holding its own, but the overall structural integrity of the car had deteriorated to such a point that it could no longer be considered roadworthy.

'Sorry mate,' the MOT inspector said. 'It's a load of scrap!'

Tim was astounded. He hadn't really expected the Anglia to sail through the test without some work needing to be done, but to be told that the only thing it was good for now was scrap metal, wasn't at all what he had been expecting to hear.

'It can't be that bad, surely?' he said, almost echoing the words that Bill had used four years previously when he was told much the same thing. 'It drives really well and looks pretty solid on the outside.'

'It's not the outside of this car that worries me. It's what's been happening underneath it that's the problem. There are some big holes in a number of structural areas and I don't think last winter helped. If you remember, we had all that snow in March and those heavy snowfalls in April. Then, to make matters worse, the snow was followed by all those floods.'

The Midlands had been particularly badly hit by the unusually late snowfalls the previous April, which were not only very heavy but led to extensive flooding in the area. Tim could remember them well, as he had needed to drive to work through the worst of the weather.

'I know the car passed its MOT when it was tested last year,' the MOT inspector continued, 'but I think the last twelve months have just about finished it off. You might get some money for it if you break the thing up and sell it off as spares, but in terms of being a roadworthy vehicle, you can forget it. There is no way that I can give it an MOT certificate and while you might find some shady garage somewhere that will be prepared to give you one, you would be taking your life into your hands to continue driving the thing.'

'Are you suggesting that bits might start falling off it?' Tim asked.

'No, that's not what I'm saying at all. I'm telling you that if you keep it on the road, the whole thing is likely to fall apart and collapse with you inside it!'

'Oh,' said Tim and after thinking for a moment or two added, 'I think what I'd better do is to take the car home and stick it in the garage for the time being. I'm not really sure what to do with it, so it will just have to sit there until I can decide.'

'You do realise that you will be breaking the law if you drive it away from these premises?' the inspector told him.

'That may be,' Tim replied, 'but if I do get stopped, then I will just produce my current MOT certificate which still has a few days left to run.'

'I should really take that off you and tear it up,' the man said. 'On your way then, but don't blame me if you get stopped by the police and they prosecute you for driving a car that's not in roadworthy condition.'

'I will just have to take my chances,' Tim told him.

In the event, Tim wasn't stopped on his short journey back to the house and when he got there, he drove the Anglia straight into the garage. As he stood by the up and over door and was about to close it, he looked back at the car and asked, 'So, what am I supposed to do with you now?'

Although he didn't know the answer to this question at the time, subsequent events proved that what he actually did with it was absolutely nothing at all. It still had three months unused road tax on it, which could have been sent off for a refund, but he didn't even bother to remove the unexpired tax disc from its windscreen. Even though Bill had neglected the car, he still used it on a regular basis, but as soon as the Anglia failed that MOT test, it was destined never to move again under its own power, or at the very at least, never to be driven again with Tim at the wheel.

He parked it in his garage and more or less forgot about it. It was under cover and protected from the elements, but Tim seemingly lost all interest in the car from that point on and it became a permanent resident of that garage in Hythe. It had been given a long term prison sentence, from which there wasn't any chance of parole and was condemned to spend its days in solitary confinement. Its only company being the ever attendant rust bugs, who would faithfully continue to nibble away at its structure. This period of imprisonment was to last for the next eleven years.

In 1992, Tim decided to leave Exxon and to take up a position with Atco-Qualcast Limited in Stowmarket, Suffolk, the company that manufactured the Suffolk Punch lawn mowers. This would mean moving to East Anglia and not knowing the area well, Tim had to live in rented accommodation initially, until he could find himself a suitable property to purchase. In the event, that year found him settled in a rented cottage in the village of Ixworth, Suffolk, about twelve miles away from the office in which he was working. It took him some time to sell the house in Hythe, but a potential purchaser was finally persuaded to buy it.

By this time, he had found a house he liked in the village of Stanton, Suffolk. It was originally the village hall, but a local builder had converted it into a house and was now selling it. The internal arrangement of the rooms was somewhat unconventional but it must have appealed to Tim, as he decided that this was just what he had been looking for and he bought it. A factor which may have influenced this decision was that the property had an attached flat roofed garage to one side that could provide a home for the Anglia Super.

No one will ever know why Tim decided to bring his old car up to Suffolk. By then it had spent eleven years of solitude in the garage in Hythe, so perhaps he thought it deserved a change of scenery, not that the inside of one garage looks that much different to the inside of any other garage. It may even have been the fact that it was an Anglia model and he had relocated himself to East Anglia. Whatever the reason, he clearly had no intention of parting with it at that time. The old Anglia Super was dragged onto a trailer and brought up to Suffolk, where it was unceremoniously pushed into Tim's garage in Stanton, there to continue its prison sentence.

The year was by then 1993 and Tim and the Anglia both had a new home, not that the change of location would affect the Anglia's future in any way. It had been steadily decomposing in Hythe and this process now continued in Stanton. The only difference was that Tim did get to see the car more often, as there was an internal door connecting the house to the garage and he kept a wine rack in there. As such, he would visit the garage on a fairly regular basis whereas in Hythe, he would have needed to go out of the house and lift the up and over door to gain entry, which was something he very rarely did.

Like his Uncle Bill, Tim was a great hoarder. He didn't like to throw anything away that might be useful in the future and this left him with the problem of where to keep it. Having an internal door to the garage proved to be a boon in this respect, as he could use the Anglia as a repository for all sorts of things. The Anglia Super gradually began to get stuffed full of empty jam jars, boxes, packaging, carrier bags, odd bits of plastic and wood and anything else he could squeeze into it. The only storage space that remained unfilled was the boot, but this was probably because it was locked and he couldn't remember where he had put the car keys.

The years ticked by and the Anglia became settled in its new home. Part of the reason for this was because all the air had escaped from the tyres and they were now flat. As a result, the car was now sitting three inches lower than it should have been. It literally was settling down onto the garage floor.

Walking around the Anglia one day, Tim happened to spot that the chrome trim around its offside headlight was about to fall off. Rust had eaten away all the solid metal in that area and there was nothing left to hold the trim in place. He stuck it back on with a short length of Duck tape and noticed, perhaps for the first time, just how rusty the Anglia had become. There were now gaping holes in both front wings, around the headlights and where they butted against the doors, and its outer door sills had completely corroded away. The only evidence of their existence being two lines of metal filings on the floor of the garage, immediately beneath both sides of the car.

The Anglia was now in a very sorry state, but Tim had promised to keep a roof over its head and that he had done, although this situation was about to change. Unbeknown to him, the builder who had converted the property and added the garage was not a very dedicated professional. He had taken on the project to make the maximum profit for himself for the lowest possible outlay and if this meant cutting corners and using cheap materials, then that was what he would do.

Tim had by then been living in the house for six years and much of the external woodwork round the windows and door frames was beginning to rot away. The wood used had been purchased from a salvage yard, in the interests of economy, and was probably very damp when it had been installed. This evidence was visible, not that Tim did anything about it, but what he didn't know was that the roof of the garage was just as bad. Its wooden rafters had rotted through and the only thing stopping it from collapsing was the cheap chipboard that had been nailed to it and the thin felt stuck to that to form a top covering. It would only be a question of time before the roof fell in and immediately beneath it was Tim's Ford Anglia Super.

This finally happened in 2001, during a particularly heavy rainstorm. The rotted timber in the roof could no longer support the weight bearing down on it and a large part of it fell down, to land directly on the bonnet of the Anglia. The car had been garaged and protected from the elements for the last twenty years, but now it no longer had a roof above its head and in its weakened state, it would once again have to face everything that the English weather could throw at it.

In 2002, the film 'Harry Potter and the Chamber of Secrets' was released and this featured a flying Ford Anglia in the same colours as Tim's car. The actual car used in the production was a 1962 Ford Anglia Deluxe, but its appearance in the film created a resurgence of interest in Anglias, which had been out of production for thirty-five years when the film was released. Many of the people who saw the film had never seen one before and they suddenly became popular again. If ever there was a time for Tim to sell his Anglia then this would have been it, but he still hung on to the car.

A year or so later, the overall condition of Tim's house had got so bad that he had no choice but to get someone in to sort it out. He called on the services of a friend from his days at Exxon and Colin and Larry arrived at the house to assess what needed to be done.

When they entered the garage, they were greeted by the sight of the Anglia, its front end almost completely obscured by the roof that had collapsed and fallen on top of it. It was raining hard at the time and water was pouring in through the gaping holes above the car and cascading down onto it.

'When did the roof fall in?' Larry asked.

'A couple of years ago, I suppose,' Tim told him.

'And you didn't do anything about it?'

At the time, Tim had done nothing more than to shrug his shoulders, turn his back and walk through the door to the house, closing it behind him. He didn't even bother to remove the debris covering the entire front end of what he had once referred to as the family heirloom. He literally abandoned the car to its fate and to the elements, adding further insult to injury. If the Anglia Super did in fact have a mind and life of its own, then it was almost certainly at this moment that the spark within it finally died.

## 19

## THE PRESENT DAY

In late 2019, another spark of life was extinguished when Tim suddenly died of heart failure. This totally unexpected event devastated everyone and the last thing on anyone's mind at that time was the car he had rotting away in the garage.

As the weeks passed and his family and friends began to accept what had happened, it became necessary to start making plans for the future, which would have to include clearing out the house and garage. By now, the Anglia had spent most of the last thirty-nine years in storage and from what could be seen of it, its condition was so bad that the obvious answer had to be to arrange for it to be dragged away and compressed into a block of scrap metal.

There was however another consideration. There are innumerable classic car enthusiasts all over the world and quite a number of them consider that Ford Anglias come into the category of collectable classics. They want to keep as many of them as possible on the road and the question had to be asked as to whether Tim's old Super, which he had refused to part with for so many years, could possibly be restored and returned to roadworthy condition.

One of his friends, Mick, decided to investigate this option and with the approval of Tim's family, took on the task of determining whether such a thing might be possible. The idea of his family heirloom being returned to something like its former glory was an intriguing notion and if this could be made to happen, it would be a fitting tribute to Tim's long period of guardianship.

The problem was where to start. Even accessing the car was virtually impossible, as the entire garage was crammed full of twenty-six years worth of accumulated junk. The car itself was full to overflowing with all the rubbish that Tim had piled into it over the years and the roof and bonnet were currently being used as a parking area for a large number of model aeroplanes. The boot top was piled high with more rubbish, but this couldn't be investigated properly as there was no way to reach that part of the garage. Added to which, the up and over garage door didn't work properly and couldn't be lifted to provide access to the car that way. Then there was the problem of the missing log book for the Anglia, which Tim must have put somewhere, and as to where he had hidden the car keys, that was anyone's guess.

A daunting task, but as Mick had a keen interest in old cars and time on his hands, he was determined to find out whether restoring the Anglia was a practical proposition. He knew he would need expert help to determine the viability of the car as a restoration project and contacted the Ford Anglia 105E Owners Club to ask for their advice. As it happened, one of the club's committee members lived relatively locally and was more than willing to view the car and provide whatever assistance he could.

The Herculean task of cleaning out the garage and the inside of the car began and Colin, who was caretaking the house on behalf of the family, did sterling work in terms of disposing of large quantities of accumulated rubbish. A few weeks later, it became possible to walk all the way around the car without tripping over things and to gain access to its interior. This was subsequently cleared out as well, making it possible for a detailed inspection of the Anglia to be carried out.

Lifting the bonnet, which was quite a job in itself because the catches didn't want to release, revealed a considerable amount of surface corrosion in the engine compartment. Two years of rain pouring down onto the front of the car hadn't done the engine or ancillary equipment any favours at all. The last time that the car had actually been driven was when Tim drove it into the garage at Hythe in August 1981. Given how long ago this was, there was little likelihood that the engine could be turned over now, as the piston rings had probably rusted in the bores and left the engine seized.

The car's battery was obviously useless, but there was no reason to suppose that the other equipment under the bonnet wouldn't function with some attention, as it had all been working properly when the car had been put into storage.

The inner wings generally appeared to be fairly sound, but there was no way of knowing what the plates attached to the top of the suspension struts concealed. Both outer front wings looked to be write-offs, although a repair might be possible by cutting out all the badly corroded areas and welding in replacement panels.

The 'A' pillars supporting the windscreen could only be viewed as suspect, particularly the nearside one, as the passenger door wouldn't open easily. The driver's door however, swung backwards and forwards quite happily.

Both door sills were now just a distant memory, but from the doors to the back of the car, the bodywork was amazingly good for the Anglia's age and the inside of the boot looked as if it was brand new. There was some surface corrosion on all four wheels, as the trims and hub caps had been removed and put in the boot, but it didn't look as if too much effort would be required to sort them out.

The interior of the car was better than expected, as the fitted seat covers had protected the front seats. When these were removed, the seats looked to be in good condition, with no rips or tears in the vinyl. The back seat appeared to be hardly used. The original carpets, which must have been kept covered for much of the car's life, seemed to be in good condition and the door panels were unmarked. Both windows wound up and down as they should and all in all, the interior of the car generally looked as if it only needed a good clean up.

There were a number of patches of surface corrosion on the bodywork of the car, but all the badges and pieces of chrome trim were still attached, except for the missing chevrons at the front of the wings. As such, the car was virtually complete and totally original, apart from the plated repair at its front end. Considering how long the Anglia had been off the road and to all intents and purposes ignored, there was nothing like as much wrong with it as was first supposed and the conclusion had to be that it was worth trying to save.

The log book and keys still hadn't been found but the original owners handbook was discovered in the boot. Someone had written the numbers for the Anglia's ignition and door keys on the back of it and this enabled a duplicate set to be obtained.

Two members of the 105E Owners Club came to inspect the Anglia and to give their considered opinion. They worked on the car for several hours and by the end of this time, the brake shoes, which had rusted to the drums, were released and the tyres re-inflated. With some effort, the garage door was finally opened and the car was rolled out onto the drive. For the first time in twenty-six years, the Anglia was again experiencing what it felt like to be outside.

Their joint assessment of the car's condition was that the Anglia Super was definitely restorable, but that this would necessitate purchasing a number of new panels, principally wings and sills, and that extensive welding work would be required. They recommended that the car should be advertised in the club magazine and a few pictures were taken for this advert.

The Anglia was then rolled back into the garage and the garage door shut. It had had its brief exposure to the outside world, but now there was the possibility that the Anglia Super might have a future after all and if this did come to pass, it would mean that it had escaped being consigned to the scrap yard for the third time in its life.

One of the biggest problems to be overcome was that no trace could be found of the missing log book. The Anglia was too old to appear on the DVLA's database and in order to obtain a duplicate log book from them, they would need to be advised of the vehicle's unique identification number (VIN). This number only appears in two places on Ford Anglias, one is on the VIN plate itself, which is attached to the offside inner wing, and it is also stamped into the bodywork on top of the front offside suspension strut. When the plating repair was carried out on the Anglia in 1977, whoever did the work removed the VIN plate from the inner wing and plated over where it is stamped on top of the strut. As such, there was no way of determining the car's VIN number and without it, the DVLA wouldn't issue a replacement log book under the car's original registration number. This was likely to be a major problem for any potential restorer, as the DVLA would re-register the Anglia with a 'Q' plate.

The club historian suggested that one solution to this problem might be to check out the car's engine number, as it was apparently common practice for Ford to use the VIN as the engine number up until the early sixties. As it was known that the car still had its original engine, this had to be worth checking out. Unfortunately, the number stamped on the engine block was in the wrong format for a VIN. It was just a normal engine number. The car's VIN still remained a big unknown.

A chance discovery in the house provided a possible way to overcome what had previously seemed to be an irresolvable difficulty, in that Tim's brother found the tear-off new keeper's slip from the original log book and there was nothing on it. It had never been filled in.

Back in the days when the old style log books were issued, the existing keeper wrote the new owner's name and address on the new keeper's slip and after signing it, sent this off to the DVLA. The rest of the log book was no longer required and this was often destroyed. The DVLA then issued a new log book in the new keeper's name and sent this directly to the new owner of the vehicle.

The latest system is that the existing keeper hands the new keeper's slip (V5C, Part 10) to the new keeper, as evidence of the fact that the vehicle has changed hands.

He then writes the new keeper's name and address in the log book (V5C, Part 6) and both he and the new keeper then sign the declaration on the log book (V5C, Part 10). The previous keeper then sends the V5C to the DVLA and they issue a new log book to the vehicle's new keeper. This generally takes about four weeks.

The difference being that it is now the log book that gets returned to the DVLA, whereas in the past, it was just the new keeper's slip that was sent to them. The log book for the Anglia Super hadn't been found, but the new keeper's slip had most certainly come from it.

It is known that Tim was given the original log book when he took possession of the car and the fact that he had not completed and sent off the new keeper's slip suggested that he never actually got round to registering the Anglia in his own name. If this was the case, then it would mean that Rachel was still the car's registered keeper

Mick began to wonder what the DVLA would do if they received the slip from the original log book, filled in with his details as the new keeper and signed by Rachel as its last registered keeper. Would they issue him with a new log book without asking any questions, or would they refuse to do so because their systems had changed since this style of log book was in use? This had to be worth finding out, so the tear-off slip was completed and sent off to the DVLA with a covering letter and the tax disc from 1980/1981.

The reason why Mick was nominated as the registered keeper of the Anglia was to ease the burden on the family, as they did not want to get involved in the sales process, if a buyer could be found for the car.

The advertisement for the Anglia duly appeared in the

club magazine and a couple of prospective purchasers expressed an interest in it. Everything that could be done to resolve the problem of not having the original log book had by now been set into motion and all that remained was to await the DVLA's response.

In late January 2020, COVID-19 spread to the UK. On 1st March, it was officially declared to be a level 4 incident and by 11th March, it had become a pandemic. On 23rd March, the government imposed lockdown restrictions on the entire population and all normal daily activities came to a grinding halt.

Whilst not wishing to minimise the catastrophic effect this disease has had in terms of the massive loss of life and untold damage to the world economies, it has also made it impossible to progress the sale of the Anglia, as no buyer was prepared to come out and view it while the lockdown was still in force.

Selling a car pales into insignificance in the light of the situation the world is currently facing, but it does mean that there cannot be a conclusion to this story of the 1964 Ford Anglia Super.

The DVLA is still working, but with a much reduced level of staff, so there is no way of knowing how long it will be before they can get around to dealing with the request for another log book for the Anglia.

The car still sits in the same garage that it has been for the last twenty-seven years, but won't now be viewed until the lockdown restrictions are lifted. As it has waited that long already, another few months is not going to make much difference. Should it get sold as a restoration project, or even if it just becomes a donor vehicle for spares, any proceeds will be going to the British Heart Foundation, to help further their research.

So, what fate awaits Tim's Anglia? It will be fifty-six years of age in August 2020 and its long life could be nearing its end, or perhaps it might be on the threshold of a new beginning. As Doc Brown said in that 'Back to the Future' film, 'The future hasn't been written yet'.

# APPENDIX

Did the Ford Anglia Super actually have a life and mind of its own? There are certainly a few strange events and happenings in this story to suggest that it might have done, but let's take a moment to examine each of them.

In the car showroom, Charlie said that the Anglia's boot fell on a customer's head even though he had heard the support strut's self-locking mechanism click into place. It might have clicked, but that didn't necessarily mean it was locked. Those mechanisms were very basic and it is quite possible that the lock didn't catch the first time. Most people double-check to make sure before letting go of the lid, but perhaps Charlie didn't.

When he was commenting on the car refusing to start one minute and then starting perfectly shortly afterwards, there is also an explanation for this. It takes a lot of energy to turn an engine over and for the electric starter motor to do this, it needs to draw a considerable amount of power from the battery. For this reason, it has to be connected using heavy duty wiring, but it would not be practical to use heavy duty wiring all the way back to the ignition switch. In order to resolve this problem, car manufacturers fitted a solenoid between the ignition switch and the starter motor.

A car solenoid is basically an electromagnet, in that

wire coils surround a metal rod that is a permanent magnet. When power is applied to these coils, this rod moves and in doing so, closes a switch. It is this switch that completes the electrical circuit between the battery and the starter motor and this is all done using heavy duty wires. The wiring between the ignition switch and the solenoid connections doesn't need to be heavy duty, so standard wiring is used.

Solenoids do 'stick' on occasions, even on new cars, and when this happens, the switch to connect the battery to the starter motor isn't activated and no power flows. The starter motor therefore doesn't rotate and the car obviously won't start. This could possibly be what happened when the customer tried to start the Anglia, as Charlie said that even the starter motor wasn't turning over. It is equally possible that the solenoid may have functioned perfectly a few minutes later, after the car had been jogged by people getting in and out of it and with the ignition switch being turned on and off a few times.

The customer who was apparently electrocuted by the Anglia was just that. A lot of carpets include a high proportion of nylon and that material is very good at generating static electricity. Back in the sixties, it is quite probable that a showroom carpet would be made mostly out of nylon. A build up of static electricity in the body happens when it passes through the soles of shoes and cannot be dissipated quickly. If a charged person then touches something that does allow the static electricity to discharge instantly, then he experiences an electric shock.

Both the customer and Charlie were resting an arm on the Anglia at the time and if they inadvertently touched the bodywork of the car with their hands, the static electricity in their bodies would have discharged instantly, giving each of them a shock. The material used for the soles of shoes can affect the build up of static electricity in the body and if Charlie was wearing shoes with leather soles and the customer had rubber soled shoes on, then it is quite probable that the severity of the shock received by Charlie would have been much less than the one suffered by the customer.

Moving on to the extra miles on the speedometer in the Anglia. Bill dreamed of being driven around in the car on the Sunday and its mileage was subsequently checked on the Monday morning. Speedometers in those days were purely mechanical devices. The gearbox drove a cable which was directly connected to the instrument gauge on the dashboard. The speed at which this cable rotated depended on how fast the car was travelling and gearing in the speedometer converted this to a proportional deflection of the pointer in the gauge, thus indicating the car's speed. The rotation of the cable also turned other gears within the speedometer to allow the number of times it actually rotated during a journey to be measured and displayed by a mechanical counter, to show the actual mileage travelled.

This mechanical system couldn't really go wrong, unless the cable or any of the gearwheels broke, so it is totally impossible for the displayed mileage to increase unless the car actually moved the distance shown, namely thirty miles. What may have happened though is that whoever wrote down the delivery mileage in the Boss's book simply made a mistake. The reading may have shown forty-eight miles, but he misread the four as a one, having only glanced briefly at the milometer, and recorded it as eighteen miles.

Did the Anglia jump for joy, as Deidre suggested, or did Bill's foot slip from the clutch because he was driving a new car and wasn't yet used to the Anglia's pedal positions? Which do you think is more likely?

An interesting point about the car's horn sounding during the attempted theft of the Anglia, apart from the fact that Anglia Super's didn't have an alarm system fitted, is how many people actually heard that horn? Bill and Deidre's bedroom was right at the front of the house, so they would have been woken up by a car horn blaring out in the middle of the night. Similarly, none of the neighbours heard anything either. Both the thieves were drug users, like quite a few of their generation in the sixties, so the one with the crowbar was not only on a high, but was also in a state of heightened excitement because he was in the middle of trying to steal a car. A car alarm going off at that moment was the one thing he dreaded most and in his addled brain that was exactly what he thought he heard.

There was no horn sounding, but he was convinced that one was. His mate had not heard anything at all and was confused when his arm was grabbed and he was hurried away from the scene, but something had spooked his buddy and he wasn't about to hang around to find out what it was.

So how did the Anglia know the location of the left luggage office ticket and the fact that it would lead to the three suitcases crammed full of stolen money? This is even more bizarre when you consider that the robbery took place seven years before the car was actually built. The answer is that the Anglia only drove to the bus stop in Bill's dream, rather than in real life, and as everyone knows, absolutely anything can happen when people are dreaming. Besides ...... You should know better than to believe everything you read in a book!

## ABOUT THE AUTHOR

Mike Turvil is a retired pension consultant, who lives with his wife in Suffolk. He studied at Hampton Grammar School in Middlesex and left there in the early sixties to pursue various different careers before becoming a financial adviser. He has a wide range of interests, which include model making and cookery, and enjoys reading many different book genres. The inspiration to write his own stories came from the works of authors such as Douglas Adams and Terry Pratchett, who he lists amongst his favourite authors, and he likes to try and capture some of their off-beat humour in his own writing.

His books are written as fun adventures, with plenty of surprises and humour thrown in. Adults will also find his children's stories entertaining and end up chuckling at some of the impossibly crazy situations Mike creates.

# ADVENTURES IN A BOND

by Mike Turvil

A humorous account of a teenager in the sixties and the adventures he had with his first car - a bright red 1954 Mark C Bond - a three-wheeler in a very sorry state.

He didn't have much money and probably even less mechanical knowledge, so it became a constant battle just to keep his car on the road. He finally convinced himself that the Bond had an evil side to its nature when it launched an all-out offensive in its campaign to drive him round the bend. There could only be one winner, but who would it be?

This amusing story of Mike's adventures with his Bond will take readers back to a time when life was a lot less complicated and the roads were nothing like as busy as they are today. To an age when the most essential bit of equipment in any car mechanic's toolbox was his big hammer and teenage tearaways were let loose in three-wheeled cars on their motorbike licenses.

Printed in Poland
by Amazon Fulfillment
Poland Sp. z o.o., Wrocław